Raining Cats and Cats

Cats

Maggie Pill

Raining Cats and Cats-Copyright©2023 Peg Herring

Editor: Trish Zenczak
Copyeditor: R. Hodges

ISBN: 9781944502515

Chapter One

Lorilee

Like an ancient Indiana Jones, I crept slowly through palmetto, climbing fern, passionflower, and other native Florida plants. Unlike Jones, I wasn't seeking treasure. I was looking for my part-time cat Bruiser, a recalcitrant, muscle-bound former tom with six toes on each front foot and the freebooting spirit of Captain Jack Sparrow.

Age, a damaged hip, a weak arm, poor hearing, and an unreliable sense of balance hindered my quest. Added to that on this morning was ground saturated by the fifth-largest hurricane ever to make landfall in the U.S. Though it had come and gone, the air still felt heavy, and moisture collected in my armpits and ran down my backbone as I swatted branches and leaves aside. I was more than uncomfortable, but I needed to find the old jerk and make sure he was okay.

Warned that we were directly in the path of Hurricane Ian, people in the greater Tampa area had braced for disastrous damage. A late turn sent the worst of the storm in a new direction, sparing us a little. We'd had plenty of hard rain and high winds. Tampa Bay had dropped alarmingly when a reverse storm surge sucked seven feet of water out to sea on Wednesday, only to send it back on Thursday.

When all that was over, we'd breathed a collective sigh of relief and returned to normal life. Stores opened again. School was scheduled to resume tomorrow. Agencies dedicated to doing good were mounting relief efforts for areas to the south that had been hit hard, such as Fort Myers Beach and Sanibel Island.

Bruiser had stayed inside during the worst of the storm, but as soon as the driving rain stopped, he'd sneaked out. At dusk the night before, I'd caught a glimpse of him sitting atop the low stone wall that fronted my property, sniffing the breeze with relish. I'd called from the patio but failed to lure him back inside. Fully aware that he was being naughty, he'd jumped off the wall and slunk out of sight.

When he hadn't shown up by morning, my imagination took over. What if Bruiser had become disoriented in the mess the storm left behind? What if he'd been hit by a falling branch or sucked into turbid water?

And the storm-drenched landscape wasn't the only threat. My neighbor, Mitzi Talbot, hated my cats and demanded they stay in the house. Bruiser, an accomplished escape artist, recognized no rules but his own, so he went pretty much anywhere he pleased. That made him an annoyance for me and a target for Mitzi and her ten-year-old son, Nasty Greg.

Two years earlier, when I started taking in stray cats, Mitzi had decided I was turning into "a crazy cat lady." After enduring months of her gossiping about me and lying about my cats, I'd lost my temper and thrown a couple of clumps of dirt in an attempt to get her to leave my property. Mitzi's response had been to sue me for "attacking" her. While the lawsuit was dismissed, I was ordered to complete an anger management course. Mitzi had bullied the homeowners' association until they decreed I could keep the number of cats I had at the time, eight, but only if they stayed in the house.

In Mitzi's tiny mind, she'd won, both in count and in the development. Furthermore, she believed that once the "unpleasantness" was over, we could again be the best of friends, which we'd never been. I'm not saying I'd unplug Mitzi's life support to charge my phone, but I would definitely consider it.

While Mitzi sought my company almost daily, I avoided hers like she was the latest variant of the COVID virus. Since she'd appointed herself Monitor of Lorilee's Cat Population, Bruiser's love of the outdoors was a problem, even at times when we hadn't recently suffered through a hurricane.

Mitzi believed she was meant to rule the world, and I envied every person she had never met.

With those dangers in mind, I'd put on my rubber boots and gone out to look for Bruiser. If he was being his usual, independent self, I'd try to tempt him back inside with treats and ear rubs. If he was in trouble, I'd do my best to help.

Pushing aside a palmetto branch that dumped its store of rainwater on my elbow, I called softly, "Here kitty-kitty-kitty!"

No meow. No flutter in the salvia leaves. Was he lying somewhere, hurt, maybe dying? What if he'd encountered Nasty Greg? *If Mitzi's kid hurts my cat, I'll teach him that kneecaps are a privilege, not a right.*

Let's not dwell on the negative, Missus Riley. That was Gunter, my anger management coach. His voice remained in my head, though our twice-a-week sessions had ended some time ago. While I'd hated being ordered to take the course, I had to admit that Gunter provided helpful ways to cope with disagreeable people. *Don't let a situation escalate*, he'd counseled. *Peace requires less sarcasm and more silence.*

The problem was that I *liked* sarcasm, and I was actually pretty good at it.

In order to please Gunter and abide my neighbors' presence, I'd taught myself to say almost nothing when Mitzi started talking. To satisfy my need for retaliation, I formed cutting responses in my head. It worked pretty well, allowing me to appear to smile at Mitzi as I savored my clever but unspoken insults.

Finding no sign of Bruiser in the yard, I picked up some downed palm fronds and bits of detritus and tossed them into the wheelbarrow. On the patio side of the house, I got a chair out of the shed, where Jess had stored them so they wouldn't become flying objects during the storm. Sitting down, I removed my boots and banged them together, sending chunks of mud flying in all directions. Once the sun dried things out a bit, I promised myself, I'd search for Bruiser again. At the moment, I had to see to the other cats.

Several of them waited in the kitchen with faintly accusing looks on their faces. "Sorry breakfast is late," I told them. "Blame your buddy Bruiser, who has no sense of responsibility to the rest of us."

7

I started in on my job as Provider of Sustenance, wet food for some, dry food for others, each in a bowl designated for them so I could keep track of quantities. One of my cats, Albert, had a weight problem, so I worked to keep him from finishing whatever the others left behind. It was a constant struggle, and Albert didn't appreciate my efforts one bit.

Once everyone else was chowing down, I took a bowl of food and fresh water to the back bedroom, where my Siamese, Maew, slept. When I opened the closet door, I saw that she lay completely still. Too still to be breathing. Touching her, I found her stiff and cold. Maew was dead.

My first thought was that Jess would want to know.

After years of having no one to share my joys and sorrows with, a seventeen-year-old boy had become my ward and my friend. Despite Jess' odd-colored hair and multiple face piercings, we'd bonded in our mutual fondness for cats. When I learned that he'd run away from an unhappy home, I'd arranged, with his parents' reluctant permission, for Jess to live with me. We'd adjusted to each other fairly well, though I had fewer leftovers in the fridge with a growing boy in the house. It had taken me a while to remember there was another human being around. Cats don't care how a person looks, but these days I tried to remember to comb my hair before leaving my bedroom, so I didn't scare the poor kid.

Jess worked for the local veterinarian, Doctor Ahuja, and that morning, the two of them had gone to Fort Myers to rescue animals lost or abandoned in the storm. Knowing he'd want to know, I texted: *Found Maew dead in her bed this a.m.*

Almost immediately I got a return text. *wht hpnd?*

I replied with a question mark, and Jess texted a sad face, adding, *hm by drk*. It was natural for the boy to ask how Maew died, since Jess planned to become a veterinarian, but it wasn't important to me. Cats can die suddenly due to heart, lung, or other organ failures. Since most of mine had a rough start in life, I was happy with whatever good time I could provide them, whether it was years, months, or even weeks. We'd seen no sign that Maew was in pain or distress, which I counted as a blessing.

If I ran things, we'd all leave this world that way, in a comfortable bed, with our bellies full and our loved ones asleep nearby.

I would miss seeing Maew on the top shelf of the etagere, as still as a statue, watching Lesser Beings move about below her, but there were other cats in need of a forever home. I couldn't do anything about it on a Sunday, but tomorrow I'd visit the shelter, and Jess and I would choose our next cat friend together.

Putting Maew in one of the biodegradable boxes I'd bought for the purpose, I took her outside, where I put my boots and raincoat back on, got a shovel from the tool shed, and approached my own personal pet cemetery.

After my husband died, I'd allowed the east side of my lawn to return to natural plants. It lessened the area I had to mow and allowed the environment a bit of its own back. In my "jungle," I buried cats that crossed the Rainbow Bridge, adding a small marker with each one's name etched on it. Tromping through the still-damp foliage, I chose a spot near the fence and began digging a hole at least two feet deep, as state law required.

By the time the hole was deep enough, my body was sore and my arms were shaking from effort. To give myself a break, I did another circuit of the yard, rubbing my back and looking for Bruiser's tracks in the rain-moistened flower beds. Along the fence, I pushed aside azalea and angel's trumpet branches to see if the old boy was hiding behind a bush. No sign of the jerk.

The sun had burned away the clouds, and its warmth felt good on my shoulders. Still, I was sad about losing Maew and scared about Bruiser's absence. I wondered if I dared sneak around the fence and do a quick search for him in the Talbots' yard. It was still early, so they might not be out and about yet.

That's when I heard Mitzi Talbot talking on the phone. She sounded dramatic, as always, but for once the situation was neither imaginary nor self-inflicted.

"I know it's Sunday, but I've got to talk to Mr. Avery," she said forcefully. "My son is at the police station, and I'm afraid they're going to arrest him."

I confess that my first thought was that they'd finally caught Nasty Greg being nasty. *Good. He'll get what's coming to him.*

Her next words ended thoughts of revenge—I mean, justice—for me and my cats. "Chris would never do what they're saying. I need to reach Mr. Avery—" Mitzi's voice broke. "Tell him to please, *please* call me as soon as he can."

I heard sobs, a vigorous nose-blowing, more sobs, and then the rumble of a sliding door. She'd gone back inside.

Chris Talbot was in police custody? That was interesting, but I had a job to get done.

Going back to the hole I'd dug, I set the box at the bottom, said goodbye to Maew, and filled it in. I made one more circle through the jungle before going back inside, achieving nothing but more mud on my boots.

As I hung up my rain gear, I thought about what I'd overheard. I didn't know Mitzi's older son very well, though he seemed to be the opposite of his little brother. Where Greg was outspoken, Chris was silent—sulky, even. While Greg was always on the lookout for new ways to get into trouble, Chris spent his free time in the driveway, working on an old Chevelle he'd bought. His greatest sin, my neighbor Art Fusilli said, was disturbing our peaceful neighborhood on weekends by inviting his friends over to drink beer at the dead end.

The Selwyn Oaks Housing Development sat along the edge of Cole Swamp. At one time the street had gone into the wetland for about a quarter mile, but to prevent trash dumping, local authorities had installed sturdy posts and a large mound of dirt, making Buckley Lane a cul-de-sac. My house was the last residence, with the wetland on its east. The Talbots lived west of me, the Fusillis across the street. The lane had been widened to a circle at the end, so vehicles had room to turn around at the barrier. Local teens had discovered that the small circle made a convenient, fairly private, place to meet. Art blamed Chris for that.

Chris and his friends had begun parking their cars at the turnaround on Saturday nights, pointed out in case they needed to make a fast getaway. "They disable the security light, roll down their windows, and turn up the music so they can dance or jam or whatever they call it these days," Art had told me. Of course there was beer, and it got pretty loud.

For me, with hearing loss and a bedroom at the back of the house, the parties had never been a problem. Art had tired of the noise, not to mention the beer cans and trash left behind, and being Bryan Talbot's boss, had demanded that Bryan and Mitzi call a halt to Chris' partying. As far as I knew, Art got his way.

If Chris was at the police station, I guessed he'd been caught with alcohol, maybe driving drunk. End of story, as far as I was concerned. I had a dead cat and a missing cat to think about, so the problems of a teenage rebel didn't amount to a hill of coffee beans.

To cheer myself up, I decided to make a batch of shortbread. I set up the mixer, which resulted in plenty of interest. Callie, my calico, perched on a Colonial-style dinette chair, watching as if to judge my baking skills. Special Ed, a gray with gold eyes and not a lick of common sense, sat next to his dish, in case I decided to provide more of his favorite food, CatPow. May and her kitten Mayson posed like bookends in the kitchen doorway, the only difference between them being Mayson's missing eye. Fat Albert and Professor Higgins slept on chairs by the sunny living room window, as usual. It took a lot to move those two from their favorite spots.

"What sort of new friend would you like?" I asked as I mixed butter and vanilla. "Do we want young or old? Friendly or in need of understanding?" As the mixer spun slowly, I added sugar, then flour. "Jess says Doctor Ahuja has rescued quite a few from that awful hurricane."

Nobody responded, but I knew they'd be fine with whatever Jess and I decided. Well, the Professor wouldn't be, but he hates everyone.

11

That evening I watched the local news, which is about all the news I could stand to know. As I munched on shortbread, which had turned out perfectly, I learned that Mitzi Talbot's trouble with her son was much worse than some drunken teenager's stunt.

Tragedy today in the town of Linville, southeast of Tampa. A car pulled from Heron Lake was found to have the body of Linville teen Ricky Fulmer inside. Police are still investigating the incident, but a source inside the department tells WatcherNews that Fulmer and another person had apparently burgled a home in Tampa. On their way back to Linville, the car, which was traveling at a high rate of speed, slid on a rain-slicked bridge, went over the side, and landed in the lake. The driver apparently escaped the sinking car, swam to shore, and fled on foot. Ricky Fulmer, who would have turned eighteen on Thursday, drowned.

The video that accompanied the report showed police pulling a dripping vehicle out of a picturesque lake. When I saw the "Linville Football" decal on its bumper, I realized I'd seen the car many times as I walked by my neighbors' home. It was Chris Talbot's '70s-era Chevelle.

Chapter Two

Jess

Doc Ahuja and I spent Sunday picking up stray cats and dogs to bring home to his veterinary clinic and animal shelter, Purr-fect Pets. As soon as the worst of the storm passed, Doc had sent out the message that he'd accept as many displaced animals as our shelter could hold. He'd treat their injuries, feed and house them, and try to locate their owners.

Before Ian hit, organizations like Wings of Rescue had removed some shelter animals, taking them to safer places. Now that the hurricane had destroyed several local animal care places, relief workers needed somewhere to house those found during cleanup. Doc had already made two trips south, loading his SUV with cages of various sizes and visiting rescue stations, where he gave emergency treatment and, at the end of the day, brought unclaimed dogs and cats back to Linville to continue their care.

It had taken me a while to convince the doc to take me along. "It is bad, Friend Jess," he'd told me. "One sees it on news reports, but it is most disturbing to actually see the wreckage of so many lives."

I insisted I could handle it, so on his third trip, Doc took me along. We arrived just after sun-up, and it was already hot. The sky above was screened by clouds, but on the ground there was so much devastation it was hard to believe it. Though cleanup had begun, there were boats where boats shouldn't be, cars where cars shouldn't be, and buildings flattened like stepped-on shoeboxes. In many areas, only the palm trees rose above eye level, still standing because they were able to bend and not break.

We spent the day driving to areas that were accessible, meeting with rescuers, and helping where we could. We came home with seven animals: four dogs, one with a broken leg; two cats, one stray, one feral but pregnant; and a parrot. I laughed aloud when the bird floated down from a tree, landed on a parking meter beside me, and said, "Hello, Pretty

Boy." A few hours later, he wasn't quite so amusing. He never shut up, so over and over, we heard, "Marlins rule!" and "Boo, 'Bama!"

"He will calm down once he feels safe," Ahuja said, but he sounded more hopeful than certain.

"Boo, 'Bama!" the bird responded from the back of the car.

At the shelter, Doc and I set about getting our latest arrivals settled. While I got the newcomers bedded down and fed, he x-rayed the dog's broken leg so he could do surgery on it Monday morning.

"Go home, Friend Jess," Doc said when he finished. "You have school tomorrow. You need rest." I thought he needed rest too, but the doc never seemed to tire when helping animals.

"If you can put the dog in the cage I got ready for him, I'll just have the mouthy parrot left to see to. Then we can both go home." I'd closed the bird in one of the storerooms, since his constant chatter irritated me and riled the other animals. While we didn't have many bird clients, I located a box of seedcakes and, on a high shelf, an old birdcage I cleaned up for him. Once I'd put food and water in the cage and lined the bottom with paper toweling, I unlocked the gate of the cat carrier we'd used to transport him and set the two openings together. After a quick look around, the bird stepped willingly into his new home and went directly to the bowl. Taking a quick drink of water, he began pecking hungrily at the seed cake. "Marlins rule!" he said between bites.

On impulse I asked, "What's your name, bird?" He looked at me for a moment, head high, as if to ask what right I had to that bit of information. "What's your name?" I repeated.

"Howie's a pretty bird."

"Howie?"

"Howie's a pretty bird."

I had the urge to stroke his shiny, blue-green feathers, but we didn't know each other well enough for that yet, so I simply echoed what he'd said.

14

"Yes. Howie is a pretty bird." Tossing a towel over the cage, I ordered, "Now go to sleep, pretty Howie."

As I walked home to Lorilee's, I realized that I was in fact very tired. With work, school, and helping with upkeep on the house, I often felt like there was always something I should be doing. Despite that, I was happier at that moment than I'd been in a long time.

Working at Purr-fect Pets was great. I'd started there as a night staffer and cleaning person, but when I moved in with Lorilee, Doc Ahuja had changed things around. Now I worked afternoons, helping with patients the last few hours of the day, which gave me practical experience and paved the way for my future as a veterinarian. At five, when the staff went home, I cleaned the place, following a schedule I'd made for myself that made sure all areas got a deep cleaning at least once a week. At nine, I locked up and went home. We monitored the animals via cameras set up around the building, which any of us could access on our phones.

Lorilee's invitation to live with her had taken a ton of pressure off me, and while I sometimes think about home and wish things had been different, it had become so hard there that I couldn't stay. It was a little weird sometimes, living with someone so old—Lorilee didn't know jack about music or movies—but she was pretty cool. And she was a great cook and baker. She made the best snickerdoodles ever.

On weekends, I helped around the house. Before we met, Lorilee was in a car accident that injured her and killed her husband. I earned my keep by doing the chores she found difficult due to her age and condition. The only time we ever disagreed was when Lorilee ignored her limits, and that was usually when a cat was in trouble. For example, the kitten, Mayson, had a tendency to shoot out any open door if he got the chance. Once outside, he immediately climbed a big live oak at the corner of the house. He had no trouble going up, but since he only had one eye, his depth perception wasn't great, so he was afraid to climb back down. He'd sit up there, shaking and crying for help.

Now, common sense should tell a seventy-something person with physical issues not to climb trees, but if I wasn't home, Lorilee got the ladder out every time. "I couldn't leave him up there," she'd say when I shook a finger at her. Luckily, young Mayson had reached neutering age in September, and the surgery had greatly reduced his desire to escape into the wild.

Lorilee had a reputation as a grump, but that wasn't exactly true. She did tend to avoid people whenever possible. She had her groceries delivered and her other supplies mailed. While she could talk for hours about cats, she found other kinds of chit-chat tiresome. She hated gossip, whining, and nosiness. People like Mitzi Talbot, who was prone to all three of those things, caused Lorilee to choose pets over people most times.

Some thought it was odd that Lorilee had installed a seven-foot privacy fence at the sides and back of her property, but once I got to know Mitzi and her Mini-me Greg, I saw why Lorilee needed that fence. Since I'd come to live there, Mitzi had tried a couple of times to pump me for information about Lorilee, but I'd given her one-syllable, unhelpful answers. She was probably convinced I was nearly nonverbal, but if it protected Lorilee, I was okay with that.

Work was great. Staying with Lorilee was good. Two-thirds of my life was happy.

School, the other third, was weird, like school tends to be for guys like me. I'm one of the weirdos at school, not a genius child, not a jock, not social. I don't care who's got new kicks or what somebody drives. I've always been a loner. Since I wasn't attending the school where my dad was principal this year, things were kind of better. That didn't mean high school was a bed of roses.

Lorilee and I had looked at two alternative schools in the area, but neither appealed to me. One was for the arts, not my thing, and the other catered to teens ordered by the court to either get a diploma or go into some kind of lockup.

With no other options close by, Lorilee had suggested I try the local public school, Linville High. Though I'd been reluctant, my first month had been mostly okay. I saw students who rolled their eyes because my hair, about an inch long at the moment, was dyed purple. Others looked away from my pierced eyebrow and lip. But at least I wasn't the only weird-looking kid there.

At the private school I'd attended the year before, I'd been the strangest-looking kid, but that was on purpose, to embarrass my dad. All my life, I hadn't been enough for him: not "manly" enough, not "assertive" enough, not "sporty" enough. Dad's constant pressure and Mom's whiny, "Your father's just trying to help you become a better person" had eventually driven me away. At Linville I was happier, even as one of the uncool crowd, than I'd ever been as Principal Pall's kid. I was polite to anyone who spoke to me, but I kept to myself. Staying nice but separate, I'd made it through my first month with no major incidents.

Then our science teacher put us into groups and assigned us to come up with a project to test a product advertised as healthy and determine if it actually was. A girl in my group, Kacie, suggested we get a variety of sports drinks to see which ones really did replenish electrolytes after physical activity. Three of the five in the group, including me, were willing to do that, but the other two let us know, in no uncertain terms, that they weren't thrilled.

Erin, a Brainiac who held her nose high like she couldn't stand to look at us, announced that she hated group projects in general. "I'll end up doing most of the work myself, so this 'project' doesn't drag my GPA down." She made air quotes around the word. "Teachers like group work because it means fewer papers for them to grade, but my mother says the school board should require that each student does his or her own work."

Yeah, Erin, because life is all about working in total isolation.

She wasn't all wrong though, because the other negative participant was exactly the type of student Erin dreaded. Lazy, loud-mouthed, and dumb, Rooster Kalamaris announced that he didn't intend to contribute. Though I didn't say so out loud, I guessed old Rooster had no clue what an electrolyte was.

Kacie's idea was good, so we went with it, ignoring Erin's snooty attitude and the fact that Rooster put his head down on the desk and appeared to be napping. When Kacie made a list of what we'd need to test the different sports drinks, I said I could borrow some of the testing equipment, since I worked at a vet's office.

Rooster raised his head to peer at me. "What do you do there?" His tone hinted that my answer would be ridiculed, whatever it was.

"I mostly clean the place," I replied, "but I help the vet sometimes, so he'll let us borrow what we need."

Rooster slid his desk back a few feet, like I smelled bad. "You clean up dog poop. That's impressive."

"Shut up, *Gerald,*" Kacie said firmly. I guessed Rooster didn't like her using his real name, because he sank into a sulk. We returned to setting up our project, but I knew I'd been pigeon-holed.

After school, Rooster passed my locker. "Oh, look," he said loudly to his friends. "There's Doggie-doo." As they passed, I heard him explain the nickname. So much for doing better in a new school.

The next day, as I approached the building, Rooster and his buds stood at the double doors, waiting until the last possible moment before going inside. "Hey, there, Doggie-doo," he called.

Though I didn't look directly at them, I had a sense of five, maybe six guys, all bigger than me, all eager for someone to harass. Since any one of them could have pounded me into butter, confrontation didn't seem like a good idea. Rooster leaned against the handrail and stuck a foot out to stop me from entering. "I said good morning, Doggie-doo. Are you too rude to answer?"

"Morning."

"How was the kennel cleaning last night, Doggie-doo? Did you collect lots of poop?"

I was considering turning around and finding a different entry point. It would only delay things, but what else could I do?

Then a voice said, "Let him by, Rooster."

Turning, I saw Chris Talbot, leaned against the wall at the opposite side of the doorway. Mitzi's older son was a senior, like me, but an All-American type, with blond hair that always looked a little tousled. I'd wondered a few times how long it took him each morning to achieve that look. The first day of school, I'd seen him in the hallway with his buddies, all wearing t-shirts that said, "Linville Athletics." Though we'd met once during the summer, so far he'd ignored me at school. If one of his friends made a comment about "the purple kid" in a tone that wasn't complimentary, they all laughed.

I'm used to it.

When Chris spoke, Rooster looked at him, surprised. "What's this freak to you, Talbot?"

Chris shrugged. "His name is Jess, and he's my neighbor."

"So you *like* your new neighbor." Rooster made it sound dirty. "That don't mean nothing to me."

"He isn't bothering you, so knock it off."

There was a pause as everyone in the vicinity thought things through. My brain screamed, *Get by while you have the chance,* but Rooster hadn't yet moved his foot. I'd have to step over it or around it, which either way would put me in a position where he could kick my butt. It was sure to get a laugh from the onlookers.

Rooster glanced at Chris, his expression confused. He'd been having fun, and if I was any judge of character, he didn't have the mental capacity to understand that he'd done anything wrong. The other kids seemed to be trying to decide whose side they'd choose if Rooster and Chris went at it.

Of everyone there, only Chris seemed unconcerned. I got the sense he'd have no problem going forward, however Rooster decided to play it.

The slightest drop in Rooster's shoulders revealed he'd chosen not to stand against Chris. He moved aside, muttering a word I chose to disregard. Hurrying inside, I went directly to my first class, avoiding, for the moment, any further chance of confrontation. I dreaded going back into the hallways after class, but no one said a word to me. In science that afternoon, Rooster acted as if nothing had happened between us—in fact, he acted as if I didn't exist.

Though I was grateful to Chris, I wasn't sure why he'd done it. After school, when I saw him leaving the building, I tried to make eye contact as a way of saying thanks. Chris seemed not to notice.

In the week since that incident, I hadn't run into any more trouble. Still, it felt like a big cloud of "maybe" hung over my head each morning when I set off for school. When would someone like Rooster, or even snotty Erin, turn their nastiness on me, I wondered, and what should I do when it happened? That was why, though work was rewarding, and life at Lorilee's was good, I wasn't willing to say that school was going to turn out well in the long run.

Arriving at home, I stepped into a world with cat toys in every corner, cat hair on most surfaces, and cat behavior on full display. At least there, everyone was glad to see me.

Lorilee was full of news about a burglary and Chris Talbot's car being found in a lake with a dead kid in it. It was pretty shocking, but to be honest, I was more concerned with poor Maew being dead and everyone's favorite bad boy Bruiser being missing. Those were things that mattered to me.

Chapter Three

Lorilee

After Jess left for school Monday morning, I felt down. The day was cloudy and overcast, with rain looking possible though not predicted. The temperature had cooled to 67 degrees, which for me meant putting on a sweater. Jess' stories of what he'd seen in the hurricane-wrecked area south of us made me sad for people without homes, businesses, and at the present moment, hope. Bruiser remained MIA, though Jess had made two forays in search of him, one the night before and another that morning. He'd had no better luck than I had, returning with muddy shoes, damp pantlegs, and no cat.

Each time I passed the living room, my eye was drawn to the etagere where Maew had spent most days, still as a statue and rigidly unwilling to allow any object to rest on the shelf with her. Sad to think that our imperial Siamese princess was gone forever.

Even the phone call I'd overheard between Mitzi and the lawyer's office stuck with me, making me feel almost sorry for my irritating neighbor. Her son's behavior had apparently gone far beyond the usual teenage misdeeds, and while I had little use for Mitzi, a kid is a kid. They do things they shouldn't. Sometimes it turns out okay; other times, as in this case, it had not.

I put the soggy, muddy clothes from our unsuccessful attempts to locate Bruiser into the washer and added soap. When he did come home, I promised myself, I'd be very stern with him. I'd find out how he got outside and I'd plug up every exit. I'd—

I'd do nothing of the kind. Bruiser was Bruiser, and I loved him exactly as he was: irritating, conceited, and...I couldn't bring myself to call him *homely*, so I substituted *unique*.

Around eight-thirty, several official-looking vehicles came down Buckley Street and turned in at the Talbot home. I was repairing my wind-battered bushes out front, so I had a slant view into their yard. A uniformed officer took up a post on the front porch, apparently on guard, while a half-dozen people put on coveralls and went inside. A gray van with police markings backed up close to the entry, and a woman paused to open its back doors before following her companions into the house. Noting their careful observance of procedure, I guessed that a search warrant had been served.

Ashamed of myself yet unable to resist, I fussed with the bushes longer than necessary, watching the goings-on next door. Two men I'd met a few months earlier, Detective Law and his frequent assistant, Deputy Brilli, arrived in their respective cars. Brilli wore a uniform and came in a squad car, while Law wore a suit and drove an unmarked vehicle. Brilli noticed me and raised a hand in greeting. Law was either preoccupied with the search or unwilling to acknowledge my presence.

Having stalled as long as I could pruning one small potentilla, I went back to my yard and worked in the flower beds. After a while I heard doors slam and different vehicles start up and pull away. When someone cleared his throat close by, I turned to find Deputy Brilli in my driveway. He was young, perhaps thirty, and slightly built. Wiry red hair curled around the brim of his hat. He rested a hand near his gun, probably from habit. "I have a couple of questions, Ms. Riley, if you don't mind."

I set my shears in the wheelbarrow. "Sit down on the patio, Deputy, and I'll get us a snack."

Brilli's eyes lit, though he glanced cautiously over his shoulder. Detective Law's car was apparently out of sight, because he said, "Sounds good to me."

In the kitchen, I plated some shortbread and poured two glasses of tea, both sweet. Setting everything on a tray, I went back outside, where Brilli sat with his legs extended. He'd deposited his hat on the table and set his phone within easy reach.

"My neighbors seem to be having a bit of trouble," I said as I set his tea in front of him.

"Could be big trouble for the older kid," Brilli acknowledged. "I need to know if you heard him leave home Saturday night."

"I'm afraid not. Mitzi says he was sick."

"My mom might have thought the same thing about me from time to time," he said with a snicker. "Parents don't know."

"You were looking for evidence that he was in that car Saturday night, yes?"

Brilli bit off a corner of shortbread. "We'll find it."

That told me they hadn't done so yet. "No water-soaked wallet in his bedroom, then?"

He shook his head. "A smart kid leaves his ID at home when he goes out to commit a crime."

"What does Chris say?"

"Keeps repeating he did nothing wrong."

"But you're sure he did."

With the air of someone who's seen it all, Brilli nodded. "He'll tell us eventually. He's not as tough as he thinks he is, and Jim knows how to get the truth out of punks like him."

Picturing Detective Law's sober countenance, I agreed, "I'm sure he does."

Brilli finished his shortbread, slurped the last of his tea, and stood, dusting the crumbs from his uniform shirt. "Thanks for the snack, Ms. Riley. If you hear anything that might help our case, be sure to call."

I cleared the patio table, setting things back on the tray, and was about to go inside when I caught sight of Mitzi. She stood in my gateway, looking most unlike herself. She wore an old bathrobe that was tied cockeyed.

Her hair hadn't been combed, much less styled. Without makeup, her eyes looked smaller, their color dim against her white face.

She apparently wanted to talk to me. It had to be done in person, because since the lawsuit, I didn't answer her phone calls. My niece the attorney had arranged for a court order that precluded any Talbot stepping foot on my property. All Mitzi could do was stand there until I noticed her. Seeing that I had, Mitzi gestured frantically for me to approach. I hesitated, unsure if I wanted to deal with Mitzi in crisis. She was hard enough to stand when things were going well.

"Lorilee, can I—" Mitzi paused, and I guessed she would have liked permission to come into my yard. I must have appeared forbidding, because she changed it to, "Can we talk?"

I didn't want to. I wanted to use my sarcastic skills and make fun of her in my head, like I usually did. But that seemed cruel today. Mitzi was a mess, and I knew at least part of the reason. Taking a few steps toward her, I asked, "What do you need, Mitzi?"

"Chris is in trouble. They pulled his car out of some lake yesterday, and they say he left his friend inside. He drowned."

I pretended I'd heard nothing about it. "That's awful."

"He didn't take his car out Saturday night, Lorilee. He stayed home, like he promised his dad and me he would."

I thought of Brilli's statement that a teenager's promise wasn't worth much. "Where were you?"

Mitzi gestured vaguely toward the northeast. "Bryan, Greggy, and I went up to Tallahassee to visit my aunt. It was her birthday, so we took her out to dinner and then spent the night. Chris didn't feel good, so I said he didn't have to go if he promised to stay in the house."

I spent my career working for the Florida Department of Children and Families. I'd dealt with more than a few untruthful kids, as well as naïve parents who refused to believe their kid would lie. Seeing Mitzi's sad face,

I didn't say what was in my head. *Kids lie to Mom and Dad. They consider it a given, a necessity that allows them to grow up and make their own decisions.*

After a little gulp, Mitzi asked, "Did you maybe hear someone in our yard Saturday night?"

"No, sorry."

Her mouth skewed sideways. "Chris had his headphones on, so he didn't either. But someone sneaked in and took his Chevelle."

"How would they get the keys?"

"They were in the visor." Mitzi pursed her lips. "A person doesn't expect thieves to come right into his yard and take things that don't belong to them."

I recall someone coming into my yard to "rescue" a few of my cats. But that wouldn't be wrong in your book, Mitzi, because it was you.

"Might Chris have loaned someone his car?"

She made a negative *pfft*. "Are you kidding? He won't even let his dad or me drive it. He worked so hard to get it running before school started, and he's so proud—" Her voice broke. "He *was* proud of it. Now it's at the impound lot, evidence of a crime—no, lots of crimes." Mitzi's tone rose, and she wiped away a tear.

I'd heard the news reports, but that didn't compare to having the mother of the main suspect in my driveway. Taking a step toward her, I said, "Start at the beginning, and tell me everything."

Mitzi seemed to calm a little at the prospect of having someone willing to listen to her. "We left for Tallahassee Saturday around one. Chris promised to stay home. He went to bed around ten—like I said, he was sick—and he woke up Sunday morning when that Detective, James Law, came to the door. They'd found his car in the lake, and...the boy who..." Mitzi paused to compose herself.

"I'm sorry."

She nodded, acknowledging my concern. "Chris texted us right away, and we started for home, because the detective couldn't question him without a parent present. Bryan took Chris to the sheriff's office, and I stayed here with Greg. I called our lawyer, who met them there." Her voice turned watery. "Bryan says Detective Law thinks Chris will be referred to the Department of Juvenile Justice." She leaned toward me. "Exactly what does that mean, Lorilee?"

"It's like an arrest, but for someone who isn't a legal adult."

"Ohhhh." Now tears fell in earnest, but she didn't even notice.

"Is there evidence that Chris was driving the car?"

Mitzi shook her head. "It's his car, so his DNA and whatever is all over it. But they couldn't get Chris to say that he was driving the car when it went into the lake, so they had to let him go."

"Who else would it be?"

"It could have been anybody," she said, her wave including most of the known world.

"What do the police think the boys were up to?"

"They say Chris and the other kid, Ricky Fulmer, broke into a house in Sunset Park." She shook her head sharply. "It's all a big mistake, but Ricky's dead, so he can't tell who really helped him and who was driving the Chevelle." Mitzi's voice rose to an irritating whine. "It wasn't Chris, Lorilee."

I mouthed the usual platitudes about things working out and the police being good at their jobs. Mitzi seemed grateful for my apparent objectivity. For a moment, I was afraid she'd hug me. Pleading busy-ness, I backed away, counseling patience. It felt harsh, but I'd had all the Mitzi I could take for one day.

As I cleaned litter pans and swept up the spillage, I tried to decide if my neighbor was being her typical clueless self or if there could be a scenario in which Chris hadn't done what the police suspected. Once the house was as clean as it gets with eight cats in residence (seven, I corrected myself sadly), I made two pumpkin pies and put them in the oven to bake. Then I sat on the couch, petting Ed and trying to put what I knew into logical form. Chris' car had been used in a crime. Chris' friend was dead. Chris' trunk was full of stolen goods. It didn't look good for Chris.

When a yowl like none other sounded at the front door, I forgot all about Mitzi's problems. Bruiser was back. While his escape routes were secret, the cat always returned home like Caesar entering Rome, in full panoply and with maximum exposure. He yowled a second time, and I set Eddie aside, muttering an apology, and went to let the Prodigal in.

Bruiser sat on the porch, wearing whatever the feline equivalent to a smile is. Beside him was a bedraggled, scrawny cat with mud-brown hair and emerald eyes. It was difficult to say how she'd made it that far, but she wobbled, almost too weak to stand. Bruiser's gaze sent a clear message: *We need to help this one.*

Chapter Four

Chris Talbot wasn't in school on Monday. As I hurried through a few isolated raindrops and into the building, I found the school all buzzy with gossip about what had happened. People who probably hadn't said two words to Ricky Fulmer their whole lives claimed to be all broken up about his death. The football guys were glum, and I heard grumbles about the season being ruined without Ricky. Erin, the smart girl in our project group, had an opinion to share, as usual. "He was kind of a jerk," she commented in her usual I-know-everything tone, "but it was lame of Chris to leave him in that car and let him drown."

Being a person who doesn't stand around chatting in the hallways can be an advantage. Since nobody paid much attention to me, I picked up snatches of conversation from several different groups. The general feeling ran against Chris, not because Ricky had been all that lovable, but because a guy doesn't leave a friend behind. He hadn't been hurt in the crash, so the consensus was that Chris could have saved Ricky's life.

"He panicked," a guy ahead of me in the lunch line said, and those nearby nodded like they'd been there. "He's kind of a wuss," someone else put in. "That's why he never made first string."

The situation interested me, both because I knew Chris slightly and because of the student body's quick rush to judgment. It was like they were one creature, with one brain that never questioned what they'd heard. Come to think of it, the world is that way a lot.

At work that afternoon, I saw that our rescued animals were making progress. The dogs were settling in, the one with the broken leg better than the other one, a collie I called "Feisty" in my head. Rescued from a collapsed building, Feisty was so traumatized that he growled at anyone who came near, even though we were doing our best to make him comfortable.

The cats had been examined and treated for minor issues, but overall they seemed okay. The bird, Howie, still talked constantly, which Doc believed was a stress reaction.

"I hope he calms down," I said. "Who could stand living with a critter that talks that much?"

With his usual wisdom, Doc replied, "Perhaps someone who is lonely, Friend Jess."

When I got home from work at nine-thirty, Lorilee wasn't in the kitchen. I heard her call from the back porch, "Out here, Jess!"

She stood under the porch light, wearing rubber gloves and an apron and holding something wrapped in an old towel. As she pulled back the cloth, I saw that it was a filthy, matted cat. While felines don't usually need human help to get clean, this one had gotten into something nasty. When I got close and smelled the foul odor, I guessed it was sewage.

"This poor thing has been through a lot," Lorilee told me. "She can barely walk. I've been giving her sips of water and a little chicken broth, but she's very weak. Lost in the storm, I suppose."

The cat lay listlessly in her arms, its eyes almost closed. "I waited until she got a little of her strength back, but now she needs a bath, so she can be allowed inside."

Lorilee had put a plastic tub on the patio table and filled it with water from the hose. She was adding warm tap water from a pitcher. Testing the water with her wrist, she nodded, satisfied. "I don't know how she'll take this."

"Let me," I said. "I'm used to it."

"That's probably best." Awkwardly, we traded roles. I took the cat while Lorilee removed the gloves and apron, then she took the cat back while I put them on.

Once I was ready, I held the cat for a minute to let her get used to me. Petting her lightly, I assured her she was going to be okay. She didn't seem able to care, and her bright green eyes drooped as if it was an effort to keep them open. Lorilee had spread a towel on the tub's bottom so she wouldn't panic when her feet couldn't grip its slippery surface. Slowly, I lowered her into the warm water. She tensed, but I held on firmly and repeated softly that she was fine. In the end, she didn't fight, though she quivered, unsure what came next.

"We have to get this crud off you," I told her. Squirting dish detergent onto her back, I lathered her from shoulders to tail and gently rubbed the suds in. She was a long-haired breed, so I knew it would take several repetitions to get her clean. As I rubbed her belly and legs gently, I told Lorilee, "We'll give her small amounts of food for a few days, to prevent refeeding. When a cat can't get food, its metabolism slows down, decreasing the amount of energy it needs. Its heart function, the oxygen-carrying capacity of red blood cells, and digestion all slow to help them stay alive."

I dunked the cat to rinse away the suds and then applied another squirt. "When they're starving, cats' bodies shift from using protein as the main energy source to using carbohydrates. If they get too much food too soon, their bodies release insulin, which causes a dangerous drop in blood levels." I worked on the tail, not pulling at it, but gently squeezing the suds along it.

"Another potential problem is fluid overload. Decrease in heart and kidney function can cause excess retention of fluids if carbohydrates are reintroduced too quickly. That can lead to heart failure."

"Interesting." At a hint of humor in Lorilee's tone, I looked up to see her smiling. While she couldn't have put all that into veterinarian terminology, she knew as much as I did about caring for a malnourished cat. What I learned from studying, she'd learned from adopting a long line of cats with a wide array of problems.

Though not thrilled with being wet, the cat was okay with the massage that went along with it. Lorilee made little sounds of distress as her wet coat made the cat's skeletal shape obvious. Hips, ribs, and backbone were clearly visible. Noticing cuts on her front feet, I said, "Maybe the doc should have a look at her tomorrow."

Lorilee nodded. "I'll take her first thing."

With a wet cloth, I gently cleaned the cat's head, paying particular attention to her ears, where fleas like to hide, and being careful around her eyes. The cat accepted it calmly. "I'd say she's not feral. She's used to contact with humans."

"I agree," Lorilee said, "but she's definitely not used to fending for herself."

"Ahuja will check for a chip, so we can post her information online and get her back where she belongs."

The water in the tub had turned an ugly color, but Lorilee fetched more from the kitchen tap so I could rinse away the final lather. "My gosh," she said as I poured the tepid water slowly from the cat's neck to tail. "I thought she was brown."

She was in fact pure white. Taking a clean towel, I gently dried her. There wasn't a spot of any other color. "Beautiful," Lorilee said. "I hope we can get her healthy again."

"We'll certainly try." Wrapping the cat in the towel, I held her close, sharing my body warmth. She felt almost weightless in my arms. "If she's okay with the noise of a hair dryer, I'll give her a few minutes of warm air, so she doesn't stay wet too long."

"Once she's dry, we'll give her a little more broth. Then she should be ready to settle in for a good, long sleep."

Petting the cat's damp head, I said, "It's good that you found this little girl, Lorilee. I don't think she'd have made it much longer on her own."

"I didn't find her. He did." Lorilee pointed, and I turned to see Bruiser, sitting far enough away that his giant paws wouldn't get wet. Head high and eyes alert, the old boy looked like a proud papa.

Chapter Five

Lorilee

Tuesday morning, sunshine returned. I boxed some pie and the last of the shortbread for the shelter staff, put the white cat in a carrier, and drove to Purr-fect Pets, where Dr. Ahuja graciously took time from his busy day to look her over. He removed several bits of glass from her front foot pads and applied little bandage boots that he sprayed with anti-lick product (bitter apple) to discourage her from chewing them off. He took samples, checking for feline leukemia and immunodeficiency virus, but gave an opinion in his usual, careful English. "She's a healthy, spayed female, well cared-for until recently. If you like, I will put her in the lost pets database and see what we can learn."

I thought Dr. Ahuja looked tired. "Are you okay?" I asked, and he smiled weakly.

"My health is good, but I keep thinking of all the animals still in need of help. The hurricane caused great destruction, and I fear it will be some time before families will be able to seek out their lost pets, much less provide homes for them."

"Jess says you've got cats and dogs in every corner."

"That is true. I simply cannot take more at this time."

Though I had given money to the vet's rescue efforts, I decided there was something more I could do. "If I take in some of the healthier cats, you'd have room for animals that need your skills."

"But Ms. Riley, you are limited—"

I raised a hand. "Sometimes necessity requires an adjustment of the rules. As long as we're careful about it, I see no reason why I can't take in a half-dozen temporary boarders."

He smiled widely. "You are a rare woman, Ms. Riley. Let us see what we can do."

We set about finding ways to provide for the extra cats by improvising. Ahuja's tech emptied several supply boxes from the storage area and poked holes in the sides to make them into rudimentary cat carriers. "You might want to keep these, so each cat has its own space in your house," she said, but she added with a grin, "Not that cats let humans choose where they'll spend their time."

Next, the tech showed me how to cut down the sides of a cardboard box and slide it into a large trash bag, making a serviceable litter pan. As for feeding, I had plenty of those plastic whipped cream tubs we all save for no good reason. They would make utilitarian food and water dishes. My own cats could share their toys with our guests, since there were plenty to go around.

"I can't thank you enough, Ms. Riley," Ahuja said as I prepared to leave. "I will let the people in Fort Myers know that I can now take in more cats."

Bruiser's rescue cat watched listlessly from the carrier as we loaded the back seat of my Lincoln with boxed felines. I felt giddy as a goose, both pleased and nervous at the thought of smuggling them into the house while Mitzi Talbot lolled on her side porch, completely unaware of what I was doing.

Most days at this hour, Mitzi would be sprawled on an inflatable raft in her six-foot "cooling pool," paging through a magazine and sipping at a glass of something pink. Unlike most sane people, Mitzi regularly baked herself in the sun, a believer in the outdated concept of a "healthy" tan. Today she wasn't outside, and I felt a single stab of guilt about putting one over on Mitzi when she was facing a family crisis. Still, I wasn't adding to her troubles. Though she'd have been horrified to learn I'd violated the eight-cat rule, Mitzi would never know. I turned into my own drive, where the seven-foot fence hid my actions from her view.

Backing into the carport, I made several trips, carrying cats and cat paraphernalia. I deposited the boarders in the back bedroom, which I still thought of as Maew's. She was gone, but her space would now provide temporary quarters for many homeless cats.

I set the cardboard boxes around the room, spacing them enough to give each cat a sense of territory. Beside each I set up an improvised litter box. On the other side I set two plastic bowls, one filled with water and a half-cup of kibble in the other. Once I finished setting everything up, I set my iPad on the nightstand and found a site Jess had told me about that played "feline-specific" music, designed to calm traumatized cats and help them relax. As the odd music played, I cut the tape on each box and let the cats out, one by one. They explored their new digs with typical feline curiosity, sticking their little noses into everything. Some included me in their exploration; some kept their distance.

Having done what I could for them at present, I left the room, closing the door behind me. It was time to fix lunch for my own cats, who had regarded my trips in and out with suspicion. *What are you up to?* was clearly the question. "It'll be fine," I told them. "It's temporary, and I'm keeping the guests separate from all of you." Hearing what sounded like a lamp hitting the floor in the spare bedroom, I sighed. Keeping up would be a big job with—How many cats in the house now? Fifteen.

Listening to the local news at noon, I learned that Chris Talbot had not been detained or charged with a crime. A reporter shoved a mic in his lawyer's face, and the man claimed, "Nothing links Mr. Talbot to any crimes, and he is vigorous in his denial of any wrongdoing. He did not leave his home on Saturday night. He was not part of the home invasion that took place, and he was not driving the car that went into Heron Lake."

Brilli's prediction had been wrong. The boy had not caved under Detective Law's questioning. It didn't mean he was innocent, and I didn't know how he could be.

Turning to the camera, the reporter added detail to the story. A string of similar burglaries had been going on for months in affluent sections of Tampa. Homes equipped with "smart" devices were robbed by thieves who hacked the system, turned off burglar alarms and surveillance cameras, unlocked the doors, and helped themselves to the contents. The police had questioned Chris about the earlier crimes, the reporter said, but he claimed to know nothing. The man's tone hinted it was only a matter of time until that was proven to be a lie.

Back at the news desk, an anchor wearing a professionally sad expression told viewers the details of Ricky Fulmer's death. The boy had not been wearing his seat belt, the coroner said, so he'd been thrown into the windshield when the car hit the water. The injury, though not deadly, had probably stunned him. "Young Ricky Fulmer's life could have been saved," the man said darkly, "if his companion had mustered the courage to take a few extra seconds and haul his friend to the surface." The co-anchor shook her head and added her contention that only police incompetence would explain why society couldn't find a way to punish the person everyone knew was guilty.

While I hadn't formed an opinion on the Talbot boy's innocence or guilt, I wondered briefly what it felt like to be the one a whole community believed was not only a thief, but the sort of person who'd leave his friend to drown while he saved himself.

As the final part of the story, Mitzi appeared on the screen. It took me a second to recognize that someone I knew was on TV. She'd made an effort to look good, but I thought the mustard-colored top and matching linen pants made her look haggard. Bryan stood beside her, his suit rumpled, and said nothing as Mitzi made rambling, almost incoherent claims. Her boy was no monster. Her children had been taught to tell the truth. The police would soon realize Chris wasn't the kind of kid who'd steal.

It was typical Mitzi. Her children had always been perfect, except when she herself was angry with them for some reason.

Until Jess came along, I'd been ignorant, even dismissive, of technology. Patiently, he'd shown me how much I could find out about the world without ever leaving my recliner or interacting with another human being. Once I got the hang of the internet, I'd bought myself an iPad exactly like his, so I could look up things that interested me, mostly cats

35

and cat behavior. I enjoyed a little screen time each day, picking and choosing articles to read and things to watch. I looked up exotic animals. I scrolled through pictures of kittens. And I wasted far too much time watching YouTube videos of '60s music. Songs bring back memories, so I could almost hear my then boyfriend, later husband Ben humming in my ear when I listened to "In My Room" or "Never, My Love." Sweet torture.

Jess seemed like a computer genius to me, but when I said that aloud once, he'd laughed. "Lots of kids are way better with computers than me. They don't just use the internet. They know how to manipulate what's out there."

"You mean like hacking?"

He nodded. "Getting into places they shouldn't be is like a game for them."

"But I thought hacking was bad."

"It is if you use technology to get stuff you aren't supposed to have." He grinned. "One guy I knew erased the information in the school library's database so he could keep a book he liked. Another kid fixed his absences on the school computer, so his parents wouldn't find out he'd been skipping afternoons."

"Why doesn't Google stop them?"

"It's not like that." I could tell Jess was being patient with me. "The best hackers go right to the deep web stuff."

"What's that?"

"It's the internet that isn't accessible using search engines. There are sites you pay for, sites you reach using email messages, and private databases." He shrugged. "I don't know any more about it than that."

I found it unfathomable, both the fact that there was internet beyond "my" internet, and the idea that people were willing, even eager, to use it to break the rules. Still, I told myself, criminals have always used what was available to get evil results from things that should have been good.

Kids Jess' age were born with computers all around them, so they'd coped, adapted, and mastered things that seemed like magic to me.

Using the internet portal I was used to, I went to Google and typed in "Richard Fulmer" and then "Christopher Talbot" and read the different news reports available. Not much there was new. Creeping Jess' social media (he'd said I could), I went to Tik-Tok and learned that Ricky and Chris had both played on the Linville High football team. A posed photo showed them kneeling side by side at the front of the group. I went to the school's sports site, where I learned that Chris was a second-string running back while Ricky had been the team's leading rusher. The copy writer, obviously a student, said Ricky's loss was a blow to the school's hopes for a winning season, but the team would fight to win "in Rickys' honer."

It was almost 3:00 when I remembered to go out and get my mail. My mailbox was out by the road these days, due to my calico cat, Callie, who shoved the mail back out of the slot in my front door as fast as the letter carrier sent it in. The mail was mostly junk anyway, but I retrieved my two charity appeals and an offer of faster internet.

As I turned back toward the house, movement caught my eye. Someone was sitting at the far end of my lot, on the stone wall that fronts my yard. His big sneakers were planted firmly on the public side, as if to let me know he wasn't trespassing. "Chris?"

"Hi."

It was the first words we'd ever said to each other. The kid had always ignored me, and I'd had no interest in becoming acquainted with another Talbot.

I walked toward him until we could converse without being overheard. "Are you okay?"

His answer was a bitter chuckle. "I doubt it."

"I'm sorry. I hope...I hope things work out."

Up close, I saw that he was much changed from the confident kid I'd seen coming and going from his yard. His posture was terrible, his face seemed shrunken, and I guessed he'd been wearing the same clothes for a couple of days.

He was silent, staring at the ground for some time, and I guessed he needed encouragement. "What are you doing here?"

"Mom says you used to work for the state. I wanted to ask if you know what will happen if they arrest me."

"I'm afraid the law will take your—the crimes very seriously. The thefts were planned, not spur-of-the-moment incidents, and someone died."

"Yeah." It was almost a sob. "What would happen if someone, like, knew what was going on—not all of it, but some. What would happen to that person?"

"First tell me what this 'person' knows."

"I—he doesn't *know* anything that would help the cops."

"Why don't you tell me what you think you know, and I'll tell you if I think the police would be interested in hearing it."

His response took so long that I thought he wasn't going to do as I asked, but finally he said, "Ricky and me were friends ever since I moved to Linville in my sophomore year. Then at the beginning of summer this year, it all changed."

He stopped, and I said gently, "What changed, Chris?"

"Just before school let out in June, Ricky told me I could make some money if I knew how to keep my mouth shut. I asked what I had to do, but he said I shouldn't get all nosy. From that, I figured what he had in mind was illegal, so I said no."

"Wise move."

"I didn't see him much over the summer. Ricky took a job at the dollar store—Coach Dailey hired him—so when I asked him to do stuff, he usually said he was busy." Chris shifted position slightly on the wall. "When we got back to school last month, Ricky was different. We still hung out in the halls and at football, but he acted like he was mad at me or something."

"That upset you."

"Yes and no. I've been trying to clean up my act lately, so not hanging with him outside school was kind of a good thing. But I didn't like how he treated me. I thought we were buds."

"Did you tell this to Detective Law?"

"I said Ricky and me had kinda drifted apart. I don't think he believed me."

"Did you tell him Ricky offered you a job that might have been illegal?"

"No." Chris raised a hand. "I can't prove that he asked, and I can't prove I said no when he did."

He was right. If Ricky had planned the robberies, he'd found someone else to help him pull them off after Chris refused. Since the last one had turned tragic, with Chris' car crashing into that lake, there wasn't much chance the police would believe it wasn't him in the driver's seat.

Chris rose to his feet, his eyes pleading. "Please don't tell anyone what I said. People already hate me because of what happened to Ricky. It won't help if they think I'm blaming it all on him."

"But if it's the truth—"

Chris held up a palm to stop me. "I shouldn't have told you that part. I came to ask you how it will go if they decide to charge me."

"As I said, it's serious." In an attempt to be comforting, I added, "If they haven't found enough evidence to prove you were there, maybe you're safe."

39

"Yeah." It sounded like he was trying to convince himself. "Thanks for listening, Ms. Riley."

As Chris walked past me and headed toward home, I tried to decide if I believed him or not. On the negative side, he was a Talbot. I despised Mitzi, loathed Greg, and had no respect for Bryan, but I had no experience with Chris. I'd thought him surly, but he didn't seem that way now. He seemed like a kid who didn't know what to do. I couldn't help with that.

At the fence, Chris stopped and peered around it to be sure no one in his family saw where he was coming from. Good. I had enough trouble with the Talbots without having Mitzi think I was willing to take on her kid's legal woes.

I went back to the house, where chaos reigned. The seven cats I'd brought from the shelter wandered the rooms and hallways, exploring every corner. My resident cats eyed me with varying degrees of disbelief and irritation. A black-and-white cat rolled in the planter by the door, chewing on the leaves and pushing dirt onto the floor. A tawny yellow cat had climbed to the top of the living room drapes, and it hung there as if unable to move. A tortoiseshell and a gray rolled down the hallway in what I hoped was play. And a large, tough-looking domestic shorthair sat beside the chair at the front window, staring up at Professor Higgins as if asking if he'd like company. The answer to that was a resounding no. Always.

"Who let you out?" I asked aloud, but the answer was obvious. "Callie!"

She was in her favorite spot on the couch, watching the newcomers with interest. Callie had come to me with a bag of tricks she'd learned somewhere, one of which was jumping at door knobs until she turned them far enough to disengage the latch. Naturally curious, she had apparently opened the guest room door and destroyed my neat plan for keeping temporary and resident cats separated.

I sighed deeply. "Welcome to my home," I told the boarder cats. "To my whole home, it seems."

Jess came in after work, eager to see what I'd done with our guests. He found it hilarious that Callie had ruined my plan for keeping the newbies separate. As I reheated a plate of roast pork and potatoes for him, I told the story. While my digestion wouldn't tolerate a meal so late in the day, Jess ate heartily when he got home from work, perfectly happy with nuked leftovers as long as there was plenty. I'd noticed his hoodies were starting to get tight across the shoulders, which meant he was putting on weight. Who says being happy isn't good for a person's health?

Surveying the multi-cat landscape, Jess said, "Seven rescues. Very cool."

"Their stuff is in the empty bedroom," I said, "but except for one that's hiding under the bed in there, they prefer to be out here."

"It seems to be going okay," Jess said. "There's a lot of difference between introducing one new cat to an established group and seven at once, but I don't see any real problems developing."

"I hope it stays that way."

Regarding sets of eyes under every piece of furniture in the room, Jess asked, "How do we know who is who?"

"No idea. They keep moving around, so I lose track."

"We need some sort of I.D. tags."

We thought about that for a few seconds, and then I said, "Seven cats. Seven colors in the spectrum."

"And?"

"I have a bunch of yarn I bought once for a project that never happened. We could braid it and make each cat a collar."

"Like the science class mnemonic, ROY G BIV?"

"Exactly."

Going into my room, I returned with a bag of untouched skeins of yarn. "I get these ideas that I'll become a crafter," I confessed, "but so far, the result is always another bag of stuff that will never become an artistic masterpiece."

It didn't take us long to make seven simple braids. It took a little longer to catch each cat and tie a basic color around its neck.

"There," I said when Jess had, as gently as possible, dragged the last boarder cat out from under the bed in the spare room. "Now we have names for them."

Jess pointed at each cat as he recited, "Red, Orange, Yellow, Green, Blue, Indigo, and—" He released the shy cat, who immediately ran back under the bed. "Violet."

"Good name for a scaredy-cat," I commented. "Shrinking Violet."

"If we'd been through what they've been through lately, we might be scaredy-cats too."

That brought Chris Talbot's pale face to mind. Should I tell Jess about our conversation? I sensed Chris would not want me to. "Did you know the boy who died over the weekend?" I asked.

"Ricky Fulmer? I've seen him around."

"Did you ever talk to him? What was he like?"

He smiled grimly. "Not to speak ill of the recently departed, Lorilee, but Ricky Fulmer wasn't the kind of guy who'd be caught dead talking to me."

Chapter Six

Jess

As I started for school Wednesday morning, I noticed Greg Talbot standing beside Mitzi's car, apparently waiting for his mom to come out and drive him to school. About ten, he had a permanent scowl and a shifty attitude. Lorilee called him "Nasty Greg," and since I'd come to live with her, I'd seen for myself that the kid was always looking to make trouble.

"Hey!" Greg called when he saw me. "What's going on over at Lorilee's? I saw a guy take a bunch of cat food in there yesterday."

"How do you know what got delivered?"

"There's a hole in the fence." He gave me an evil grin. "I don't know how it got there, but I saw maybe four cases of canned cat food and two big bags of kibble on the dolly the guy took inside."

I kept walking. "What can I say? Our cats like to eat."

Moving sideways, he followed my path along his yard. "You sure she hasn't got a few extra cats over there?"

"A cat is a cat. They don't come in regular and extra."

"But Lorilee can only have eight. If she's got more than that—"

I stopped and turned to face the kid. "If she did, it wouldn't be any of your business. If it was your business, I'd tell you that Lorilee has exactly eight cats." I went on, leaving the little jerk standing at the edge of his lawn. I didn't look back to see if my claim had been accepted.

It wasn't a lie if I considered the other cats mine, right?

Chapter Seven

Lorilee

Deputy Brilli and Detective Law showed up at my door Wednesday morning after Jess left for school. Seeing their car pull into the yard, I turned in a panic and began scooping up cats left and right. Hurrying down the hall, I dropped them in the guest bedroom, backing out and closing the door in their surprised faces. On the second trip, I had to crack the door just a few inches and drop the two I'd collected through while holding the ones already inside back with a foot. I only found five cats, but I figured Violet was still under the bed. That meant only one of the boarder cats was roaming free. If my visitors didn't take a head count, we'd be fine.

I hadn't talked to the detective since I'd almost been bludgeoned to death for discovering the person who'd killed a woman and dumped her body in my yard. Law had made it clear he thought I'd interfered in his investigation. In my view, Jess and I had pretty much solved the case for him. He could *think* I was a nosy old woman if it made him feel better about his investigative abilities, but he'd better not say it aloud.

When I opened the door to invite them in, I noticed right away that they looked uncomfortable. "Good morning, Ms. Riley," Law said. "Do you remember me?"

"Of course I do, Detective." I almost added, *It's only been a month and I'm not senile yet,* but Gunter the Anger Management guru cautioned silence in my head, so I didn't. "Please, come in."

They stepped into the foyer, and I closed the door behind them. Law looked into the living room and asked, "What happened to the cat that tried to escape all the time?"

"Mayson is beginning to adjust to the rules," I replied.

"That's good, right? Less trouble for you." He seemed overly interested in the house, which was about the same as the last time he'd been there: cat toys everywhere, the Professor napping on his chair and Fat Albert on his, and fine, dancing hairs floating in the air, lit by sunbeams that came through the window. Licking his lips, Law said, "How have you been, Ms. Riley?"

He was stalling, which meant he was uneasy about something. "I'm fine," I replied. "Sit down, and I'll get us some coffee. I just took a cheese Danish out of the oven. Are you interested?"

They were. By the time I'd plated the pastry and set everything on a tray, the two men had cleared seats for themselves. Law sat on the far end of the couch, leaving Callie's favorite spot empty. Deputy Brilli opted for the rocking chair, which was as far away from the Professor as he could get. The last time he visited, the cat had sliced his hand with his lightning fast, nasty claws when he tried to pet him. The experience had left the deputy unwilling to take further chances.

"Is that a new one?" Law pointed at the stray, who lay sound asleep in a basket next to my chair.

I gave them a brief version of Poor Kitty's story, ending with, "She's recovering, but she sleeps a lot. Bruiser brings her things: bits of string, a stuffed mouse, or a jingle ball. She's too weak right now to do much more than look, but he keeps trying. It's really cute."

Law agreed aloud that it really was cute. He complimented the pastry and the coffee. He even mentioned the weather before he finally got around to his reason for coming. "We need to know where Jesse was last Saturday night."

"What?"

Law wiped his brow lightly with a hand. "Can you tell us where Jess was on Saturday night?"

"He was here. We worked on a jigsaw puzzle and he did a little homework. Around ten, he went to his room."

"So you didn't see him after ten o'clock?"

"Well, no, but—" Suddenly it came to me. "Mitzi Talbot told you that Jess stole her son's car and robbed some house in Tampa."

Brilli looked out the window, as if something out there was really interesting. Law looked down at his hands. "He's right next door," he said after a few seconds. "He knew the car was available. If he slipped it out of gear and pushed it out to the road—"

"Detective, do you have any evidence Jess did that?"

"Well, no."

"Then finish your snack and go find out who really was in that car."

"Ms. Riley—"

I held up a hand. "I shouldn't have to tell you this. You know Mitzi is a born troublemaker, and she's desperate to save her son. I can't believe you're willing to entertain such a ridiculous scenario."

"If we could take a look at his room—"

I rose to my feet. "Come back with a warrant, *if* you can get a judge to give you one on the word of that—that—" I couldn't think of a word bad enough for Mitzi, at least not one I'd ever said aloud before. Going to the door, I opened it, indicating they should go.

As they passed, Brilli gave me a glance I interpreted as sympathetic. It wasn't a complete surprise, then, when he showed up in my yard an hour later. By that time I was outside, ripping weeds out of the ground as if they were Mitzi Talbot's hair.

I'd gone to her house as soon as Law's car disappeared, intending to tell her off, but her car wasn't there. Since then, sand burrs had substituted as targets for my anger, but they hadn't lowered its level one iota.

"Ms. Riley?" When I turned, Brilli put his hands out in a defensive gesture. "We didn't mean to upset you. Jim has to investigate every reasonable lead, you know that."

"It's not 'reasonable' to suspect Jess of being a criminal simply because he lives next door to the Talbots."

"Maybe not, but we also can't ignore information we don't want to hear."

"What did Mitzi tell you?"

"She says Jess came into their yard Saturday morning, looked the Chevelle over good, and asked Chris all about it."

"I doubt that. Jess is no motor-head, and besides, I've warned him about that nest of vipers, so he knows enough to stay away."

"We gotta act on what we're told, though. You get that, right?"

Setting my hands on my hips, I sighed. "I suppose."

Still, it was frustrating. I knew Jess hadn't stolen that Chevelle to commit a burglary, but it's difficult to prove that something *didn't* happen. Chris would know if Jess had really looked his car over, but if his mother was plotting ways to divert suspicion from him, he'd be smart to keep quiet and let her do it.

Honest to Pete, if Mr. Rogers were Mitzi's neighbor, he'd move.

My plan was to listen for Mitzi's return, but when I went back inside, I had a cat incident to handle. The two rowdies, Yellow and Indigo, had captured an anole lizard that somehow found its way into the house. I'd heard them scrabbling with something earlier that morning but, already used to their noisy play, I'd ignored it. In my bedroom, I found the lizard, dead and much worse for wear, on my pillow.

Cats have the reputation of being demanding, ungrateful creatures, but that isn't true. They often bring gifts to their favorite humans in appreciation for that person's care for them. *You feed me,* they mean to say. *Now I, a mighty hunter, have found food for you.*

While anole was not on my diet, it's never nice to refuse a gift. It also isn't polite to scream or retch or toss the thing across the room. "Aren't you brave?" I said brightly, keeping any trace of sarcasm out of my voice. "And you're giving your trophy to me? How nice!"

I petted both cats and ushered them into the hallway. Once the door closed behind them, I tossed the poor dead thing into the toilet and flushed. Then, unwilling to sleep with scattered anole parts that night, I stripped the bed and put on fresh everything.

The whole time, I thought about what I'd say to Mitzi when she got home. There were logical arguments: Jess was no criminal. Jess hadn't come home wet. Jess had shown no signs of trauma that would accompany an event like that. But Mitzi wasn't prone to logic, so I didn't think that would work. I might appeal to her better nature, but I wasn't sure Mitzi had one. I had to remain calm and collected while I explained, without resorting to insults, that she had to retract the things she'd said to the police about Jess.

When I heard her car pull into the drive, I thought I was ready. I'd be cool about the issue, and we'd discuss the much more likely scenario, that Chris had driven his own car that night. In the face of my cool presentation, she would be forced to admit that she was wrong.

All my best-laid plans turned to steam when I rounded the fence and saw Mitzi's plump figure leaning into the back seat to remove several shopping bags from Beall's and Kohl's. Apparently she'd treated herself to a little retail therapy after attempting to ruin poor Jess' reputation. "What in screaming blue blazes did you think you were doing?" I yelled as I approached. "You told the cops Jess stole your son's Chevelle?"

Mitzi's whole body froze at the sound of my angry voice. Turning toward me, she spoke between tightly set lips. "I was trying to be helpful to the sheriff's department. It is a citizen's duty to provide as much information as she can in an ongoing investigation."

"Helpful! You're about as helpful as a screen door on a submarine."

In my head, Gunter cautioned, *Keep your purpose in mind. Insults don't move a conversation forward.*

I tried to calm down. I tried to breathe normally, unclench my fist, and stop picturing it smashing into Mitzi's round face. I tried to keep in mind that I probably had to live next door to this woman for the rest of my life.

Unless you murder her today, a different part of my mind whispered.

Mitzi licked her lips. "I didn't mean to harm anyone. I merely pointed out a few alternative facts to Detective Law."

I managed to keep my thought to myself this time. *You are not attractive enough to be this dumb.*

"You tried to sic him on someone other than your kid."

She sniffed. "It's a possible scenario, and you can't deny it."

You'd better die on a weekday, Mitzi, because no one will break their weekend plans to attend your funeral.

"Jess has done nothing wrong."

"But he *could* have taken the car."

"He didn't, and you know it. You deliberately lied."

She pulled herself up to her full four feet, eleven inches. "I would never—"

I stuck a finger under her nose. "You did."

I should have seen it coming. After a sniff that was loud and deep, her expression went from defensive to destroyed. Suddenly, Mitzi was clinging to me, her wet face buried on my chest. "I'm sorry," she snuffled into my shirt. "I had to make them leave Chris alone."

I peeled her off me as gently as possible. "Mitzi, you can't just make things up. It's wrong. It's not helpful. And it's a crime."

"I didn't mean to. It just ... came out."

She was a mess, mascara running down both cheeks, hair mussed from our (unwanted on my part) embrace, and lipstick smeared, probably onto my shirt. "You don't know how—how—destroyed Chris is by this. He went to school this morning like there was a firing squad waiting for him there. Otherwise, he stays in his room, all sad and quiet. Yesterday I picked up his phone and saw—You wouldn't believe the horrible things the kids are saying to him and about him on social media. They call him 'Killer Chris.' They say he's going to prison. One text said he should just kill himself and get it over with."

"No."

Mitzi wiped her eyes with the hem of her shirt. "You can't believe how awful it is."

I'd heard stories of online bullying, but telling a kid he should kill himself? How was that even human?

"He's talking about quitting school," she went on, "and I can't blame him. It's brutal." Looking at me hopefully, she suggested, "Detective Law knows you. Can't you tell him Chris would never rob anyone?" Her fingers grasped my arm and pinched, and I tried not to pull away. "Chris isn't that kind of kid, Lorilee. A mother knows her child."

I didn't have the heart (or the crayons) to explain to Mitzi how naïve that was. In the first place, I had no knowledge of her older son's integrity or lack of it. Even if I did, Jim Law would not, could not, accept my opinion on the subject. "Nothing I could say will change a thing, Mitzi. We have to wait and hope things work out."

She took a final swipe at her eyes. "I suppose you're right. No police detective would let a woman twice his age tell him how to do his job."

Just when I'd started feeling sorry for the woman. *Are you naturally this dumb, Mitzi, or do you practice?*

As I returned to my yard, I berated myself for not being tougher on Mitzi. Desperate parent or not, she had no right to make up stories implicating Jess. But her meltdown demonstrated how upset she was by all this.

Her clueless final comment stung. *Why wouldn't a detective listen to someone with twice the life experience he has?*

Back in my house, with my cats to calm me and no Mitzi to rile me further, I tried to decide if Chris might indeed be innocent. He was Mitzi's kid, which was no recommendation, but when we talked, he'd seemed sincere. If the police had decided he was the guilty party and stopped looking into other possibilities, Chris was in a bad position.

"Maybe," I said to Callie, "Jess and I should look into the case a little. He could ask around at school to find out if Chris ever showed signs of criminal behavior. I've dealt with more than one teen who betrayed himself by boasting to his friends about what he'd done, so there might be rumors at school. If it wasn't Chris, Jess might hear who really was involved in those burglaries."

Callie purred to show solidarity, but I had immediate second thoughts. "No. We should leave it alone. Jess has a lot on his plate right now, so I shouldn't give him more to do. And his goal at school seems to be to stay under the radar as much as possible, so he won't want to go around asking questions." I sighed. "Mitzi and her crew will have to deal with their own troubles."

Hearing a mew, I looked up to see Poor Kitty standing at the kitchen door. "You're looking better." Gently setting Callie aside, I went and picked her up. Already she felt a little heftier, and her movements were more fluid and...well, cat-like, despite her bandaged feet.

Petting her, I looked at the chaos that was my home at the moment. With a sick cat, seven guest cats, and my own cats, I had plenty to keep me busy. Detective Law would have to see this case through on his own.

Chapter Eight

Jess

When I got my first glimpse of Chris Talbot at school on Wednesday, he looked like a completely different person. His eyes were kind of sunk into their sockets, and the muscles along his chin looked like they were stuck in flex. He stared past everyone as he crossed the schoolyard, apparently focused on something in the distance. A few kids spoke to him, but Chris seemed not to hear.

The football team gathered as usual at the main doors, and I saw one of the guys nudge the others when he saw Chris approaching. When he neared the door, the testosterone-heavy cluster all turned their eyes on Chris, giving him a group glare. Someone made a comment I couldn't hear, but it was clear that Chris did. Lips closed tight, he turned abruptly and headed around the building, to a side entrance where he wouldn't have to run the gamut of his former friends. Though he held his head high, he looked like he might spew at any second.

Welcome to the other side of high school, I thought. *You were one of them. Now you're not.*

I didn't see Chris for the rest of the day, but I certainly heard his name mentioned. Opinion had solidified against him. First, everyone could see he was uninjured, which meant, according to the majority, that he could have saved Ricky. Second, details had emerged about the burglaries, and the general consensus was that Ricky hadn't had the technological smarts to pull them off. That meant, people said with the certainty gossips everywhere have in their own stories, that Chris was the mastermind. He'd roped Ricky into his crimes and ended up getting him killed.

As I went about my day, I listened to the voices of those who "knew" what had happened and wondered if anyone would even ask Chris to tell what he knew. I doubted it. People looking for drama seldom want to hear the whole story.

Again, not my business, and not something I could help with. I went from class to class, offering no opinions when the subject came up.

To get from school to the shelter each afternoon, I cut through a narrow alley between the post office and a bar. It meant skirting a smelly trash bin and puddles of urine left by bar patrons who considered the alley an extra toilet, but it saved me half a block. As I entered the alley that day, I stopped suddenly and let out a gasp of surprise. Chris stood with his back against the brick wall of the post office. A guy of about forty had him by the shirt, telling him something in a low, urgent tone.

My first thought was to turn and get out of there, but the man heard my footsteps. "Hey!" he hollered. "What are you doing back here?"

My reply was genius, though I had no idea where it came from. Pointing over my shoulder, I said, "Detective Law is out there in his car. He sent me to tell Chris that he needs to talk to him."

A ripple of uncertainty crossed the guy's face. Letting go of Chris' shirt, he leaned in and said something in his ear. Then, thumping Chris on the chest once with his knuckles, he started off in the opposite direction.

I approached Chris. "You okay?"

He adjusted his shirt. "Fine." Looking over my shoulder, he said, "What does Law want?"

"Who?" I grinned, and he got it.

"Good one."

"Why was that guy hassling you?"

He hesitated before replying. "Just general stuff."

"Does it have to do with what happened last weekend?"

"No." He seemed unsatisfied with a simple negative. "No way."

"Okay." It didn't feel like the truth, but I didn't press. "I gotta get to work. See ya."

"Sure, dude. Later."

"Stay away from thugs, okay?"

"I'm good now," Chris said. "He had a point to make, and I got it."

When I got home that night, Lorilee was cleaning up cat pee in a corner of the kitchen. "Somebody's not using his litter box," she said as she squirted neutralizer on the spot. "I'm not sure if it's anxiety or territory marking."

"Let's hope it's new-kid nerves," I said. "We don't need a bully in the house."

Once I'd helped her finish the job, we washed up and then sat down in the living room for a while, giving affection to as many cats as possible. Lorilee told me about Ms. Talbot saying I might have taken Chris' car. I thought it was kind of funny, but she didn't see it that way.

"You could have let them look in my room," I said. "There's nothing there to link me to car theft or home invasion."

"It's the principle," Lorilee said primly. "Detective Law should know very well that you're not that kind of person."

"I would hope so, but I guess it's good that he's following other leads and not focusing only on Chris."

Holding Eddie and trailing a string across the floor for Red to chase, I told her about seeing Chris get attacked in the alley.

"It's bad enough that his former friends have turned on him," Lorilee said. "Now there's an adult harassing the poor kid?"

"People can be weird."

"If Chris did what they say, he's no doubt feeling guilty about it. And if he didn't do it, he's being judged before all the evidence is in." She sighed. "Not that it's unusual for people to do that."

I tried not to judge Chris. In fact, I tried not to think about it. If he was guilty, the police would find out and arrest him. If he wasn't, they'd arrest someone else. It was none of my business. Though I knew what it was like to walk the halls of school feeling like you've got no friends, there was nothing a freak like me could offer Chris that wouldn't make his situation worse.

Chapter Nine

Lorilee

The malnourished cat, Poor Kitty, seemed much stronger on Thursday. She tottered around at my heels, like a duckling imprinted on the wrong species, and rubbed her head against my finger when I gave her a little pâté. Once she'd shown proper gratitude, she went to work and finished every morsel.

While Jess dressed for school, I used my tablet to search for new information on Chris Talbot's situation. It was a little hard to concentrate, since Indigo and Yellow, two boarders who'd become best buddies, were in full romp. Jess complained that they'd run through the house all night, rolling and tumbling into walls. I hadn't heard them: one advantage to having partial hearing loss.

As the cats tore through the house like runaway trains, I read new details about the robberies attributed to Chris and the deceased Ricky Fulmer. So-called "smart homes" had been subjected to "brute force attack," meaning their passwords were discovered by hackers essentially guessing until they were successful. The thieves then used the home's wi-fi to make the security system an accessory to the crime.

"Except for the fact that they found the stolen goods in Chris' trunk, the police have no proof the boys were in the house," I told Jess when he came into the kitchen and splashed water over a bowl of Cheerios. He didn't like milk and claimed cereal tasted fine with water, but I was unwilling to test that claim for myself. "The theory is that the burglars wore those suits forensic evidence gatherers wear. It says here that a person can buy them for less than ten bucks apiece, so they probably tossed them into a Dumpster once they were done with them."

Jess' expression turned doubtful. "I wonder how two guys like Chris and Ricky would figure all this out? Buying those suits. Finding out which houses to hit. Shutting off security systems. It seems like a pretty sophisticated plan for a couple of jocks to dream up and accomplish."

I set my chin in my hand. "And it doesn't seem like something Chris would do, in my opinion."

"I thought you didn't know him."

After a moment I said, "One gets an impression after living next door for two years. Do you have any idea about his character?"

"I heard he was partying a lot last summer. They'd get that homeless dude that jams in the park to buy beer for them."

"Kevin the Dancer?"

"Yeah. They give him money, he buys, and they give him a few beers as a reward."

"That's bad," I admitted, "but not in the same ballpark as home invasion and fleeing the scene of an accident." Gesturing at my tablet, I said, "The press has named them the 'Home-Hack Gang.'"

"Leave it to them to give it a cutesy name. I kinda feel sorry for Chris at school. It's rough on him there, but he doesn't let his feelings show." After a moment, Jess said, "He's a little arrogant, maybe, but he doesn't seem ... What's the word?"

"Larcenous? Cowardly? Evil?" I set the tablet aside. "I wish I could pick a certain detective's brain and find out what *he* thinks."

Rinsing out his bowl, Jess set it in the dishwasher. "Law isn't going to tell you or me anything."

"No." I wriggled my brows, "But I bet he talks to his brother, and Deputy Brilli loves my cookies."

Chapter Ten

Jess

A drizzling rain on Thursday made the walk to school miserable. Lorilee had offered to drive me, but I'd refused. Getting dropped off by what looks like your grandmother isn't a good way to arrive at any school ever. Though the rain wasn't heavy, the gloomy clouds overhead added to the tiredness I felt that morning. Work the night before had been hectic and beyond noisy. Every five minutes, one of the dogs would start barking, and then the whole place would explode with sound. Each time, it took forever to get everyone calmed down.

I'd been making an extra effort to have everything set up for the next day, to make life easier for the staff. We couldn't neglect our regular patients, but we had all the rescued animals to deal with too, so Doc and his people practically ran from case to case. I made sure the surgery and exam rooms were well-supplied, and I listed items we were running low on, so the tech could order more.

Food was a big expense. Luckily, Dr. Ahuja had a good reputation and a great network, so almost every day, someone brought in pet supplies or donated money. Some, like Lorilee, opened their homes to animals healthy enough to be fostered until their owners or new forever homes could be found. The dog with the broken leg now fostered with a couple who said he was a great dog. I suspected they'd keep him if his original owners weren't found.

Despite how rewarding my work was, I'd come home the night before and dropped onto my bed, completely out of steam. While Lorilee considered her seven "boarder" cats a joke on Mitzi, payback for all the harassment we took from her, they made it harder to rest. Blue had moved in with me, which was good for him, but it was hard to understand how one seven-pound creature could occupy ninety percent of a double bed. Blue also thought that making the bed was a game, so as soon as I started that morning, he got in the way and stayed there. Since I'd been in a hurry, I'd pulled the blankets up and left him, a large lump in the middle, to find his own way out.

With all that, I hadn't had time to finish my homework for the day. I hurried toward school, hoping to get a few minutes to finish before first period began. If not, I hoped Ms. Hall would be understanding.

With all that in my head and my hood pulled close to keep the rain off, I didn't even think about Chris as I passed the Talbot place. When I picked up movement from the corner of my eye and turned, he was there, leaning against a tree. "Hey, dude."

Since Lorilee had told me how the Talbots set the cops on me, I wasn't sure how to respond. I answered "Hey," but kept walking.

Chris fell in beside me. Glancing sideways, I saw his throat pulse as he swallowed hard. His question came as a complete surprise. "Do you have any idea what it's like to have parents who are asshats?"

I slowed a little. "Actually, I do." Chris thought about that and, after a moment, nodded to indicate he understood. Kids who are happy at home don't often move in with an elderly woman and a houseful of cats.

"Right. So, my mom was going crazy trying to get the cops to believe I didn't do all that stuff last weekend, and she went too far, like she always does. My dad—He doesn't even try to stop her anymore." He sniffed. "Anyway, I'm not always proud to call them my parents. Mom told the cops—" He stopped, unable to put it into words.

"She said I stole your car. I heard."

"As soon as I heard what she'd done, I called Detective Law. I told him Mom was wrong, that you never showed interest in my car, and I'm a hundred percent sure you didn't take it Saturday night."

"Did he believe you?"

"Hard to tell."

"Well, it's cool that you tried." A few steps on, I asked, "Why'd you tell Rooster to lay off me that day?"

Chris chuckled softly. "I worked on the stupid car all summer."

"And—"

"I was outside a lot when you were helping Lorilee. You ... you're good to her. She's been alone a long time, and my mom and my monster little brother haven't made her life easy. I'd hear you joking with her and I'd think, *He's a good dude.*" He spread his hands. "So when Rooster started in on you, I just said out loud what I'd thought in my head lots of times."

"Well, I appreciate it."

We were almost to the school, and Chris said, "Dude, I'm gonna hang here for a while. It's better if I don't show up early, because ... you know. Besides, you don't need to be seen with me right now." When I hesitated, he urged, "Go ahead. I'm fine."

I did as he said, not because I was afraid to be seen with him, but because having me on his side wouldn't help Chris a bit. Unless he could prove he hadn't left Ricky to die, his reputation couldn't get much lower, whether the weird new kid in school stood with him or not.

Chapter Eleven

Lorilee

Jess texted to tell me that Chris Talbot had contacted the sheriff's department and contradicted his mother's story. It was nice to learn that Chris wasn't as sleazy as his mother. Not that it put him up with the angels. Whoever told Mitzi she should just be herself couldn't have given her worse advice.

It was raining lightly but the temperature was cool, so I went out to the front porch to sweep away the fine, thin layer of black dirt that constantly drifted in from somewhere and settled onto it. As I worked, I heard a funny noise and looked out to find Mitzi at the end of my driveway. She was dressed, painted, and powdered, her outfit all in shades of purple. She held an umbrella over her head to keep off the rain. As soon as I noticed her, her face lit with a smile, and she waved frantically, as if we were long-lost friends who'd found each other again.

Like a lighthouse in the desert. Bright, but useful to no one.

"Lorilee," she called, "I need you to go with me today. Can you be ready by ten?"

"Go with you? What are you talking about, Mitzi?"

"I want to go to Ricky Fulmer's viewing, and I'm scared to go alone." Her tone turned pleading. "I have no one else to ask."

Why would I go to the viewing of a teenager I never met ... with Mitzi? *I'd have more fun navigating speed bumps at Lowe's.*

"I'm going incognito." She indicated her plain (for her) outfit. "I'll say I'm the mother of one of the cheerleaders." She sounded a little wistful, and I guessed Mitzi would have loved having a daughter she could push in that direction.

I hesitated. Was it worth an hour with Mitzi to learn more about the boy who'd died? Public opinion had taken a "What happened to this promising young man?" slant. That question might be answered by meeting his family. Swallowing my distaste, I said, "All right. I'll be ready."

By ten o'clock, the rain was down to a mist. I'd put on black pants and a plain shirt and combed my hair into what passed for presentable. Hanging my purse over my arm, I walked over to where Mitzi waited on her porch, paging through some sort of celebrity-worship magazine.

"I want you to know that we straightened out the mistake with Detective Law," she said as we got into her car. "He won't bother your young man anymore."

If that wasn't a backward apology, I'd never heard one, but I let it go. "Good to hear."

Mitzi was a better driver than I had imagined. She made complete stops at red lights and used her turn signal. Her foot was smooth on the accelerator, and she didn't send me hurtling toward the windshield when she braked.

Everyone has one thing they can do well.

On the downside, she talked the whole way, repeating herself as if she could prove her son's innocence by litany. I said little, in need of more information before I could form an opinion. Luckily, Linville wasn't that big, so it was a short ride.

The Bellow Funeral Home was a long, low building with white vinyl siding and a dignified portico to keep the rain off visiting mourners. I was distressed to see a sign out front displaying photos of the departed, along with the hours of each one's visitation and service. I made a mental note to threaten a lifetime of haunting to anyone who put my photo up in muddy pixels on a public street after I died.

Entering through double doors, we stopped to look the situation over. The lobby was cream-colored with dark wood accents. Boxes of tissues sat on every flat surface, and organ music played softly in the background. On either side were benches I guessed were seldom used. Who sits around the lobby of a funeral home?

We stood for a moment, unsure where to go next. A slightly harassed-looking woman came out one of the doorways and approached, hands clasped in what I thought of as the mortician's pose. "I'm so sorry I wasn't here to greet you," she said. "Who is the loved one you're paying respects to today?"

"Ricky Fulmer."

"Oh, yes. So young." She gestured toward a doorway. "His friends are this way." As she led us to the door farthest from us, she said, "We have four this week, so it's been a bit of a struggle."

Each doorway had a photo (again!), and I saw that three of the four were people my age or older. Only Ricky had most of life ahead of him. That was sad, no matter what he'd done.

The woman left us at the doorway. Just inside was the visitors' book, and Mitzi went over and signed it with careful strokes: "Jennifer Elwell and Annabel Gray."

"Which one am I?" I asked.

"You're Annabel." Mitzi examined her signature. "I always wanted to be a Jennifer."

I hesitated as the reality of lying to a group of mourners set in. I guessed Mitzi felt the same, but after a few seconds, she set her lips. "Here goes." She moved toward the casket, and two steps behind, as befitted my supporting role, I followed.

Ricky Fulmer had been a good-looking kid. Standing beside his earthly remains, I wondered what had tempted him into crime. The papers had mentioned a mother but no father, and judging by the general look of those in attendance, the family was blue collar. Several of the men wore shirts with repair-shop or home services logos on the back. The women's clothes aimed for current styling but betrayed their discount store origins with cheap fabric, poor sizing, and garish trimming.

Had theft provided income the boy craved, the chance to buy tech-y toys and cool-kid clothes? Or had Ricky been one of those shallow-thinking types led astray by a friend? Deputy Brilli thought that friend was Chris Talbot.

"Split up." Mitzi spoke out the side of her mouth, like a gangster in a black-and-white movie.

"What?"

"You talk to the old people. I'll take the ones my age."

Though somewhat resentful, I did as she said. Surveying the room for "old people," I saw a man of about my age standing alone a few feet from the casket. He was tall, with white, combed-back hair, a bulbous nose, and kind-looking blue eyes. As I passed, I murmured, "Such a tragedy."

"The wages of sin is death." His voice rumbled with conviction. *So much for kind eyes.*

"Um, I suppose that's true."

"It is Truth. Romans, 6:23."

"Right."

He inclined his head at the others in the room. "They'll tell you he didn't do it, but God knows what that boy did." He glanced at the casket. "Ricky faces his judgment, even now. He will learn what I tried for years to make him understand."

I wished I'd kept my mouth shut and walked on by, but I decided to learn what I could. "Ricky was family?"

The man's chin rose, and his words came in sermon tones. "I had two grandchildren, different as night and day. One listens to the teachings of the Word; one never would." He raised a large hand, gesturing toward the casket. "Ricky reaped what he sowed, and now I have only one descendant. I believe his cousin will do better in life, since she follows the counsel of her elders and her Lord."

"That's great. I'm very sorry for your loss." I moved on quickly, leaving Saint Grandfather glaring at the world like Moses come down from the mountain. No wonder he stood alone.

A woman at least a decade older than I sat in an upholstered chair along the wall, leaning her arms on a walker. Everything about her drooped: her eyelids, her hair, the muscles of her upper arms. Pointing at a straight chair beside her, I asked, "Mind if I sit for a minute?"

Turning hawkish eyes on me, she thought about it and then nodded. "Go ahead."

Once I was settled, I said, "My daughter-in-law knew Ricky through her kids, but I don't know anyone here. I just came to keep Jennifer company." When she didn't speak, I added my stock line. "Such a tragedy."

"Yes." She lifted the seat of the walker, took out what looked like a piece of towel, and wiped her neck and forehead.

"Gram, are you okay?" A girl of about Jess' age stood before us, wearing a modest dress in navy blue. She was attractive but rather plain, with no talent, or maybe no desire, for makeup.

"I'm kinda overheated," the woman told her. "Could they turn the A/C up a little?"

"I'll ask." The girl turned to me and said politely, "I'm Ricky's cousin Dylan. Are you a friend of Gram's?"

"No," I said. "We met because we both needed to sit for a while."

She nodded. "This is all so hard, and the heat doesn't help."

"Do you go to Linville High too, Dylan?"

"Yes. I'm a junior. Ricky was a senior."

"His death is very sad."

She put a hand on her chest as if pressing her emotions back. "The sheriff's department is wrong. There's no way Ricky was involved in those home invasions, and I hope they figure that out soon."

Family is often the last to believe. Mitzi was one example, and it seemed Ricky's cousin was another. "What do you think happened?"

Again, the hand went to her chest. "I can't say what someone did or why he did it." She smiled, showing slightly crooked but very white teeth. "I try to focus on what I might be able to do that's right, not what others are doing wrong."

"Very admirable."

"Dylan has a heart for service," the old woman said. "She looks after me and makes sure I'm okay. Now, Ricky was more into school stuff, football and track, but she's right. He would never have taken what wasn't his."

"Then I hope the truth comes to light," I said.

Touching the old woman's hand, Dylan said, "I'll ask about getting you a little more A/C, Gram." As she moved away, I noticed she limped a little.

"Your granddaughter seems like a good kid."

"Great-granddaughter," she corrected. "Dylan's my granddaughter Alys' kid. Her cousin Ricky was Donna's son." She pointed out the women as she spoke, and I saw that Mitzi was talking earnestly to Ricky's mom, Donna. My companion added an opinion. "Dylan's right. Ricky would never steal. We taught him better than that."

"Then what do you think happened?"

"That other kid done it, and he picked Ricky up afterwards. Ricky had no idea what was in that car trunk." Her voice wavered. "But now he's dead and can't speak for himself, the cops are making out like he was a criminal."

I maintained what I hoped was a look of interest. "Well, it's good that you've got … Dylan for comfort."

She nodded. "Ricky was a big athlete and all, but Dylan is smart as a whip."

"She does well in school?"

"Yeah, but she's got common sense too." Her tone indicated clearly that school smarts took second place. "A few months ago, somebody started messing with my bank account. I don't like that automatic deposit they do with Social Security now, so I go down to the bank every month and get my money in cash. When I went there in … April, I think it was, there was only three-quarters of what I was supposed to have."

"How would that happen?"

"Don't ask me, honey. But I told Dylan, and that girl went on the computer and fixed it so nobody can withdraw my money anymore except me." The girl appeared across the room just then, caught our attention with a wave, and raised one hand, palm up, to signal she'd had the A/C boosted. "Dylan really does love serving others, and she's got the smarts to do it."

As Dylan moved off, I saw Mitzi looking my way. She tilted her head toward the door, and I got the hint. Rising, I said, "It was nice meeting you, and again, I'm sorry for your loss."

In the car, Mitzi asked what I'd learned. "The family refuses to believe that Ricky was involved in crime, with the exception of the gentleman who looks like a Biblical prophet."

"That's his paternal grandfather."

"He thinks the kid's going to Hell, but the great-grandmother says Chris picked Ricky up after Chris robbed that house."

67

"The mother and two aunts each told me the same thing. It's like they came up with a story and united around it."

"People believe whatever makes them comfortable. Was Ricky good with computers?"

"Not that anyone noticed. I suppose he could have kept it secret, so no one knew he was planning robberies. Chris is good with some computer stuff, but I hate that everyone thinks he—"

"Yeah, yeah. He wouldn't do it. Listen to this." I told her the story of the old woman's missing Social Security money.

Mitzi's eyes widened. "I'll bet that awful Ricky tried to steal from his Nana."

"If he did, the girl, Dylan, stopped him."

"Would she know who was taking the money?"

"She'd have to suspect. You'd need specific information to access the woman's bank account, and it sounds like a kid to me, taking a few bucks here and there."

"Would she tell?"

"I don't imagine so. She seemed pretty introverted."

What would a kid like Dylan do in that situation, I wondered. Warn Ricky to stay out of Gram's account? If so, Ricky might have looked elsewhere for a way to get money.

Chapter Twelve

Jess

After fourth period, I stepped out of the media center at exactly the wrong moment and again ended up in Chris Talbot's business. He was pushed against the lockers, held there by two big guys who seemed to be enjoying themselves. My first thought was to turn around and go back inside, like I'd forgotten something, but when Rooster Kalamaris punched Chris in the gut, I couldn't pretend I didn't see it. A group of about twenty kids clustered around them, watching, and when someone voiced approval of the first blow, Rooster hit Chris again, grinning for the crowd like the idiot he was.

"Go home and don't come back, Talbot." The guy holding Chris' right arm had a beard that would have made a lumberjack proud. "After what you did to Ricky, nobody wants you here."

"I didn't know you guys ran the school." I heard the words before I realized I was the one who'd said them. Every eye in the vicinity turned toward me. I saw relief on Chris' face, but dread too.

I couldn't believe I'd spoken. At my former school, I'd learned to be quiet and ignore what went on around me. Despite my turtle approach, every once in a while someone would notice me and feel the need to tell me what a jerk my dad was. Did they think I didn't know? While they'd drawn the line at giving the principal's son a swirly or a serious beat-down, they got back at him by making my life harder, messing with my locker, stealing my lunch, or tripping me in the hall.

In movies, the hero eventually gets righteously angry and defeats the biggest bully of the bunch, either with his fists or his wits. At that point, the other kids decide they like him better than they ever liked the mean kid, which ends the problem.

People like me know that isn't how it goes.

In junior high, I'd read dozens of articles about dealing with bullies. The usual advice was to seek adult intervention, which was, in my opinion, worse than living with the harassment. Go to a teacher, guidance counselor, or anyone else on staff, and even the non-bullies look down on you for being a crybaby.

I knew about bullies and bullying, so why had I stuck my nose in where it didn't belong here at Linville High? No time to work out an answer to that.

My reading did help a little. I kept my expression neutral, showing neither fear nor anger, since bullies want a reaction more than anything else. I made my face muscles relax, though my hands shook and my heart pounded against my ribs like it wanted out of my chest. I glanced at the circle of students standing by, hoping to find an ally or two, kids who might support Chris if I got the ball rolling.

No friendly face looked back.

Outside our little circle were students who hadn't joined in, but at that moment, every one of them seemed to find the contents of their lockers really interesting. Even if they felt bad for Chris, they wouldn't take on Rooster and the boys. Linville High had turned against one of their own, and I was the only one dumb enough to speak up for him.

Research claimed that a non-aggressive question can sometimes make a bully back off. "What did Chris do to you?" I asked.

Rooster laughed, showing small, uneven teeth. "He didn't do nothing to me. He wouldn't dare, cuz I'd kick his ass."

"Then why are you hassling him?"

He tapped Chris on the chest with a stubby finger. "Chrissy here is a thief. He steals stuff from people's houses."

"Have the cops charged him with that?"

Rooster blinked once. "No."

"Why haven't they?"

"It's one of them technicalities."

"So the cops don't know what happened, but you do."

"Damn right." He waved a hand, appealing to the group. "But he's worse than a thief. He let Ricky drown in that lake."

"Is that another technicality? Because I never heard that he got arrested for that either."

"It's the truth, smart ass. They just ain't got enough proof for a judge and that." Again, he appealed to the crowd around us, and several nodded agreement.

"If Chris punched you right now, would it prove you're wrong?"

Rooster frowned. "No way."

"Then does punching him prove you're right?"

He gave the crowd a big grin. "Nope. It just proves I don't like him."

"I think we established that, but I'm not getting why you're so sure you know what Chris did."

"If you listened, dumbass, you'd know. Everyone in the whole school knows."

"So if everyone in the whole school knows you shave your pubes because some girl said it was cool, does that make it true?"

Rooster's cheeks turned red. "That's a lie, you little weasel!"

"I heard it more than once over the last few days." I looked at the faces around me. "So I guess everyone knows."

"You freak! I'm gonna break your face."

Rooster took a step toward me, but I showed him my phone, which stuck out of my hoodie pocket, with the camera running. "I've got you on video, threatening both me and Chris. You'd better hope neither of us has an accident in the near future."

At that moment, the two guys who'd been holding Chris suddenly let go of him, stepped away, and melted into the hallway crowd. The kids who'd been watching our little drama shifted bags, purses, and books and turned away, apparently recalling places they were supposed to be.

"What's going on here?"

I turned to find the guidance counselor, Mr. Gage, standing with his hands on his hips, his suit coat spread to reveal suspenders with the school mascot on them. "Gentlemen, what's the story?"

Chris spoke first. "Rooster and I were goofing around."

Gage turned to Rooster. "Is that true?"

"Sir, yes, sir." The guy could not stop being a smart aleck.

Turning to me, the man asked, "You're new here?"

"Yes."

"Name?"

"Jess—Jesse Pall." I shuddered, hoping he didn't recognize my last name from administrators' conferences with my dad.

If he did, Gage didn't make the connection. With the blindness typical of petty bureaucrats everywhere, he made a decision. "Detention after school today. All three of you."

Chapter Thirteen

Lorilee

The noon weather report said the temperature would be in the mid-70s, so I figured I could walk to Purr-fect Pets, deliver some snacks, and be back home without breaking a sweat.

Before Jess came along, I'd walked almost everywhere I went. I'd gotten into the habit of dropping off goodies to the shelter staff a couple of times a week, since I appreciate them and love to bake. There's no way I could—or should—eat as much as I make, so I became the snack lady for the people who did so much for cats.

Though I'd managed to overcome my dread of driving, I still liked walking. It's good for a person, and without the additional weight of baked goods, the walk home would be less taxing.

I didn't stay long at the shelter, since the staff was inundated with work. A grumpy man informed everyone that he was waiting for his dog to be brought out from the back. "I haven't got all day," he muttered loudly enough for everyone to hear. A worker came out with the dog, a pretty little collie, on a leash. "That's him," the man said. "Gonna put him to work keeping looters away from my stuff." I felt a little sorry for the dog, but it wasn't my business. Setting the plate of baked goods on the front desk, I waved to the receptionist, who was speaking into the phone, and left.

As I got close to home, I caught movement at the gateway to my house. Frowning to get a better view, I saw a figure slip out the gate, around the fence, and into the Talbots' yard. Greg.

What had he been doing in my yard? If he'd peeked in my windows, what had he seen?

By the time I reached him, Greg stood near his front door, trying hard to look innocent. "Good morning, Mrs. Riley," he said in a fake-polite tone.

"Greg."

"How are your cats today, Mrs. Riley?"

"As well as can be expected, I suppose. Why aren't you in school?"

"Parent-teacher conferences," he said. "We got out at eleven." He took a step toward me. "I was wondering, what would happen if one of your cats had babies? I mean, you can only have eight, right, but if one had three or four or whatever babies, what would you do about it?"

"I don't take in pregnant cats," I replied. "If one shows up, we take it to Dr. Ahuja."

"Then I guess you don't have to worry about having more than eight cats in your house, right?"

He had been peeking. Keeping my voice level, I said, "Why would I worry?"

"The homeowners' association said eight cats and no more. What if they called Animal Control, and you had to choose which cats to give up? I bet that would be hard."

His tone, his face, his whole being irritated me, but that wasn't unusual. "I don't worry about things like that, the same way you don't worry about violating the judge's order about trespassing on my property."

That gave him pause, but I saw the wheels turning in that evil little head. He couldn't admit he'd spied on me, but he intended to figure out a way to let somebody know about my boarders. It was only a matter of time.

Chapter Fourteen

Jess

For anyone who hasn't served detention since *The Breakfast Club* was filmed, it's pretty much the same. When classes finished at 2:30, Chris, Rooster, and I were expected to bring class work of some kind and show up at the media center. We were the only three rule-breakers that day, so we shuffled in together, avoiding eye contact.

With most of the students gone, the room was cooled almost to chilly, with tables of varying sizes scattered around the center. Along the walls were shelves and shelves of books, though I wondered if anyone actually read them. There was a bank of computer stations, but they'd been turned off for the day. On the wall above the windows was a banner, probably twelve feet high, that said, "Linville High School - Demanding Excellence."

The door closure was broken, so it slammed behind me. When I jumped at the sound, Rooster wheezed a laugh and muttered something that sounded like "Loser."

"Put your phones in the organizer," Mr. Gage ordered. "No internet during detention."

I was behind the other two, so I saw that while they pretended to obey, Rooster and Chris each put something into one of the phone-sized plastic pockets that was not a phone. I guessed they'd done this before and knew that the guidance counselor didn't check to see that they'd complied. While I hadn't planned ahead, I improvised, sliding my wallet into the slot. It made an acceptable bulge, and Gage seemed satisfied.

"You were told to bring work. Let's see it." I had a veterinary science book Doc Ahuja had loaned me, which got a grudging look of approval. Chris had a classic cars magazine. Gage frowned but didn't comment. Rooster had come empty-handed and defiant. "I don't read for fun, and I got no school work worth doing."

"Well, you're not allowed to sleep or talk, so get a book off the shelf." Gage glared at him, adding, "Expand your mind a little."

With a sneer that dared Gage to object, Rooster looked the opposite way as he drew a book from the nearest shelf. Strutting to a desk near a back corner, he dropped it on the desktop from three feet and then slammed his body into the chair so hard that it slid backward and hit the wall with a crack. I chose a table as far away from Rooster as I could get. Chris distanced himself from both of us.

"Two hours, gentlemen," Gage said, glancing at the clock and writing down the time. "We don't tolerate fighting in our school, no matter who starts it."

"Makes perfect sense," Chris said sarcastically. The proctor scowled at him but didn't reply.

I tried to immerse myself in the book I'd brought, but Rooster was determined to see that didn't happen. About every three minutes, he had a question. First it was, "Can I open a window?"

Gage, who was working on his laptop, replied with a terse, "No."

"But Ms. Dormer said in health class today that indoor air is way more polluted than outdoor—"

"No, Mr. Kalamaris. Read your book."

"Oh, right." He examined the back cover. "*The War of the Roses.* I gotta tell you, so far it's fascinating." A few minutes later: "Can I use the bathroom, Mr. Gage?"

"No."

"But I gotta *go*."

Gage looked over the top of his glasses. "You've been here less than ten minutes."

"But I didn't want to be late, so I didn't stop on the way. And—"

"No, Mr. Kalamaris. Read."

Just when I got back into the procedure for determining if a lump on a cat's leg is serious: "Mr. Gage, what did you do on your summer vacation?"

The man sighed. "Mr. Kalamaris, shall I extend your detention?"

"Geez, I was just asking. I'm very interested in you, sir."

Flushing, Gage decreed that Rooster would stay an extra ten minutes in detention for that interruption and ten more for each additional one. That ended the questions, but to compensate, Rooster began making annoying noises. He tapped the window with his knuckles. He dragged his tennis shoes across the floor, making the rubber soles squeak. He hummed. When Gage looked up he'd apologize, as if he'd been unaware, but as soon as Gage (and I) tried to get back to work, he'd come up with a new irritation.

With a sigh that hinted he knew it would do no good, Gage finally rose from his seat and went to where Rooster sat. Leaning over the kid, he spoke in a low tone, the man-to-man approach. In a much louder voice, Rooster claimed he was trying to behave. "I'm AD/HD," he said, his face a mask of fake innocence. "I can't sit still for very long, but it ain't my fault."

A sound to my right drew my attention, and I saw that a small paper airplane had landed next to my book. It was a page from Chris' magazine, but in the margin was a phone number. I glanced at him, and he nodded to encourage me. Nodding back, I took out my phone and held it under the tabletop until Gage returned to his chair and went back to work. Making sure my phone was in silent mode, I added Chris' number to my contacts and messaged him: *??*

A few seconds later I got a reply. *Thx 4 tryg 2 hlp.*

Was he making fun of me? Criticizing my lame attempt at intervention? I looked his way, but he appeared intent on his reading.

A few minutes later, a knock on the door brought me out of my veterinary science book yet again. With a beleaguered sigh, Gage rose and went to answer. Through the opening, I saw a square-built girl of about my age wearing a t-shirt with Shakespeare's picture on the front and gray jogging pants. Reddish-brown hair fell to her shoulders in large waves, and while her face was in the shadows, I guessed she had freckles. The straps of a backpack showed on her shoulders, and I imagined her getting ready to leave school for the day but then deciding she needed to talk to Gage. The set of her chin hinted at determination, and a glance in my direction indicated that her purpose had to do with me.

The girl gestured for Gage to come into the hallway, which he did. Rooster immediately called across the room, "Hey, new kid. You better erase that video you took."

I met his gaze. "It's in the cloud now. If you bother me or Chris again, I'll take it to the cops."

"They won't do nothing." He didn't sound confident.

"I guess we'll see."

Rooster called me a name. Taking out his phone, he made a call and began telling someone what a pain detention was.

Through the long, narrow window in the media center door, I watched the girl tell Gage a story that took a while. She gestured a lot, her body language revealing a strong desire to be heard and understood. Forgetting my book, I watched as Gage's manner went from irritated to interested. My theory that the girl had come about the fight was borne out when she pointed at each of us in turn. Meeting my eyes, she gave me a little smile, as if to encourage me to be strong.

I smiled back, signaling that I would. She was kind of cute, and after all, it was detention, not prison.

When the girl finished what she had to say, Gage turned to look at the three of us. Rooster had put his phone away and sat with his hands clasped in his lap, the picture of innocence. As he re-entered the room,

Gage said something to the girl, who said what looked like "Thank you" and left.

"We've been here an hour," Gage announced. "I'm releasing Mr. Pall and Mr. Talbot from detention. If you encounter further trouble from Mr. Kalamaris, come immediately to my office, and I will handle it." To Rooster he said, "As for you, young man, we have rules about bullying. A further incident will result in you being banned from sports for the rest of your senior year."

Rooster started to fuss, but Gage raised a hand, signaling that objections were useless. Chris reacted first, rising from his seat and retrieving whatever he'd substituted for his phone from the rack. As he headed out the door, I followed, but Gage stopped me. "Why are you reading that book, Mr. Pall?"

"I'm planning on veterinary medicine as my career."

"Good for you," he said. "Come by my office next week, and we'll see what you need to do to get started."

Though I didn't know Mr. Gage, the joke at school was that getting students into college was his thing. "Don't tell him your troubles at home," people said. "Don't ask for help with a teacher who makes your life hard. Filling out apps and FAFSA forms is all that makes the guy happy."

"Thanks." By the time I got my wallet and left the media center, Chris was gone. I'd hoped to talk with him about the incident with Rooster, the message by paper airplane, and the text, but it was time for me to be at work. I'd texted to say I'd be late, but since my detention had been cut short, I could get there before closing and get updates on the day's concerns.

As I left the building, the girl who'd talked to Mr. Gage waited on a bench near the door. "Hi."

"Hi." After a pause, I asked, "Did you have something to do with getting us sprung from detention?"

"I told Gage what happened."

"You were there?"

She shook her head. "Word got around. I heard you made Rooster look like the jerk he is."

"Gage didn't seem to care which one of us is a jerk."

She shrugged. "Gage isn't a bad guy, just a little lazy. It's easier to punish everybody than to try to dig the truth out."

"Why did he believe you?"

"I work in his office one period a day, so he trusts me."

"Well, thanks. No one else saw a need to set the record straight."

"People love drama."

"I don't."

"Most do." Sounding bitter, she added, "Why look for the truth when a lie is so much more fun?"

That sounded like something personal, but I didn't know her well enough to ask for details. "Why'd you stand up for Chris?" she asked. "Are you and he friends?"

"Not really. We're neighbors, but there's this thing between his family and my guardian, so we don't talk."

"What thing?"

I shook my head. "It was before my time, but I guess his mom is a little ... different."

She gave me that crooked smile. "I hear that. You can't pick who you live with."

It didn't feel like a good time to mention that I'd picked Lorilee, or at least that we'd picked each other. "I, um, I have to be at work, so...I gotta go."

"Where do you work?"

"For the vet at Purr-fect Pets."

She bit her bottom lip. "I'm going that way. We could walk together as far as Coral Street, if that's okay."

"Sure." I could feel my neck getting red. "My name's Jess."

"Hi, Jess. I'm Wendy Byrd. Everyone calls me Birdy, like the Wendy Bird."

That took me a minute. "From *Peter Pan*, right?"

"Hey, that's pretty good."

"It's about as far as my literary references go, I'm afraid. Kids' books and *Star Wars*."

Looking at me in mock seriousness, she announced in a deep voice, "You are young, Skywalker. There is hope for you still."

I don't remember much of what we talked about on our first walk together. Birdy seemed like someone I'd known forever, and it was kind of like the day I'd first talked with Lorilee. It was even better this time though, because instead of bonding with a senior citizen, I was getting to know a girl with big, brown eyes and a warm, kind of crooked smile.

Not that bonding with a senior citizen is a bad thing.

Chapter Fifteen

Lorilee

Jess had relayed Nasty Greg's gleeful comment about a hole in my fence, so late Thursday afternoon, I went outside to find it and see that it didn't serve his purposes ever again.

My yard was looking beautiful. I have flowers in as many places as possible for as much of the year as possible, which in Florida is most of the time. Along the admittedly ugly fence I'd placed all kinds of plants, beautifying the wall that in turn supported the plants. I started at the street end, where lilies bloomed in yellows and oranges, and worked my way along to the back, gently pushing aside branches of azalea, floribunda, and Rose of Sharon.

There was no obvious hole, no hint of daylight from the other side. Turning around, I returned more slowly, running my hand along the wood at about the height of Nasty Greg's eyes.

There it was. A knothole shifted slightly when my hand passed over it. It was about two inches wide, and it tapered on my side, so if I'd pressed firmly, I could have punched it out and sent it onto the grass on the Talbot side. I guessed Greg had loosened it with a jackknife blade, so he could remove the knot when he wanted to peep and set it back into place when he was done.

Going to the toolshed, I found a thin board and cut a piece about four by four inches off with a handsaw. Taking my power drill, I returned to the fence and screwed the board into place over the hole. I used the shortest screws I could find, so they wouldn't protrude on the Talbot side and spur complaints of booby traps.

Replacing the drill, I cleaned up the mess, satisfied for the moment but sure I hadn't ended the problem. How long, I wondered, before Nasty Greg outgrew his fascination with harassing me and trying to deprive me of my cats?

When I got back inside, the house was quiet. That was nice, but anyone who has multiple cats will attest that it's also ominous. A quick check of the house showed minor damage—the toilet paper in my bathroom almost completely unrolled across the bedroom floor, and a small puddle of vomit, mostly bile, in the laundry room doorway. After taking care of those items, I sat down in my rocker to read a little. Immediately I was joined by Callie and Ed, so I made room for them on either side. Three others, Orange, Mayson, and Indigo, curled up nearby and napped.

As I tried to read, my mind kept returning to the death of one teen and the assumption that another was to blame. Had Chris panicked and left his friend to drown? I didn't know enough about him to say. Still, what I'd sensed in his behavior wasn't guilt. It seemed more like fear, and perhaps frustration.

If he was indeed not the one who'd been in the car with Ricky, it was up to Chris' parents to support him and defend his innocence. The problem with that was that neither of them was very bright. Mitzi thought her statement that Chris wasn't guilty should be enough to make the police look elsewhere. And as far as I could tell, Bryan hadn't said a word about the situation.

In the few times I'd met him, Bryan Talbot seemed to me a man who simply ignored whatever unpleasantness he encountered in life. A pompous platitude, an ambiguous sniff, and another beer, and he was done coping. Even the lawyer they'd hired to defend Chris was a mistake, in my opinion. The guy dealt in wills and divorces. What did he know about police procedure and protecting the kid's rights?

"It's too bad," I told Callie, combing her white neck with my fingers. "I'm no expert, but I think I could have done better if Chris were my son."

Chapter Sixteen

Jess

I couldn't wait for school on Friday, and it was the first time I'd felt that way in probably a decade. School meant I'd see Birdy again, and while we had no classes together since she was a junior, I figured I'd track her down at lunchtime. As I showered and got ready, I worked on what I'd say.

"Oh, hey, Birdy. How's it going?" Was that casual enough?

"Birdy, hi. How are your classes today?"

"Brilliant," I told the bathroom mirror. "You could also wear a sign around your neck that says, 'Loser.'"

For a second time, Chris was waiting on the sidewalk past his house, and he stepped in beside me. "Dude, it was pretty cool how you took Rooster on yesterday."

"You made him leave me alone before. I tried to return the favor."

He grinned, and for a second he looked like the old Chris. "It was kinda dumb though. Rooster's a little nuts."

I flashed my own grin. "Yeah. Guess I lost my head."

He frowned. "That's twice you stuck your neck out for me. You got a death wish or something?"

I raised my hand like I was swearing an oath. "If it makes you feel better, I'll promise never to come to your rescue again."

"Deal." A few steps on, he said, "I'm glad Birdy told Gage the truth."

"What do you know about her?"

Chris gave me a look I couldn't read. "Are you two together?"

Why was he asking? Suddenly Birdy's intervention showed in a new light. What if she'd gone to Gage to get Chris out of trouble? What if she'd just meant to be polite when she walked with me and let me go on about animals and stuff?

I shrugged. "Never met her before yesterday. I wondered why she made the effort."

"Girls. Who knows what they're thinking?" Chris pushed back a lock of hair that had fallen onto his forehead. "Birdy's super smart, and she's nice, but she's ... different, you know?"

"A loner?" *Like me,* my brain said. A second later, it cautioned, *Two loners don't necessarily make a couple.*

"She studies, like, all the time. Says she needs to get scholarships, because her stepdad's got no money to send her to college."

"I see."

"She has a lot to do at home too," Chris said. "They kinda treat her like she's the maid."

"How do you know?"

"Back when I first came to Linville, Birdy and I had first hour together. I thought she was cute, but she could never go anywhere or do anything. She had to have supper on the table at six. She did all the shopping, ran all the errands. Saturday mornings, she hauled clothes to the laundromat and sat there for hours while they washed and dried." He shook his head. "Once I got to know other people, we kind of drifted apart, because there was no time for fun in Birdy's life."

"That's not right."

"The stepdad works all the time, and—Hey!" We were about to cross a street, but a car came around the corner without stopping at the sign, so we had to jump back. "Jerk!" Chris hollered. When it was gone, he said, "Nice wheels, though."

I chuckled. "You really are a gear-head. Somebody almost runs us down, and you notice the car."

"Dude, if I could wrench on cars all day, I'd throw away the whole rest of the education system."

"No plans for college?"

"No. Mom thinks I could be a Senator or mayor or whatever. Pa thinks I'll get some job where I wear a tie every day." He made a dismissive noise. "I talked to a rep from an auto tech college up in Tallahassee, but I haven't told the 'rents about it yet." He turned. "You got plans?"

"Veterinary school."

"Cool." I could tell from his tone he didn't get it, but that was okay. We all do what makes us happy. At least, we should.

Again Chris stopped a block before the school. Across the street, two girls approached from a different direction, and he turned away, avoiding their notice.

"That's Ricky's cousin Dylan," he said. "I'd just as soon not meet up with her, so I'll wait here a while."

I continued on alone, watching the girls ahead of me and trying to decide which one was related to Ricky. Both wore loose tops with ripped jeans and sandals, but I thought the one on the right bore a family resemblance, thick brown hair, high cheekbones, and a sprinkle of freckles across the nose. As she stepped off the curb, she favored her left foot.

I remembered Lorilee saying she'd met Dylan at the funeral home. She'd seemed dedicated to helping others, and she'd been concerned for her grandmother's comfort. While I hadn't known Ricky well, I thought that while the cousins might share genetic similarities, they had very different personalities. Up ahead, Dylan laughed at something her friend said, and I liked the sound of it.

Birdy stood in front of the school, scanning the incoming crowd. Her backpack again bulged with books, and she again wore sweatpants and a t-shirt, this one with Neil DeGrasse Tyson's picture on it. When she saw me, her eyes, which I'd noticed were hazel most of the time, turned greener and kind of sparkly. I thought—hoped—it was me she'd been waiting for.

It was. Dragging me to a spot where no one could overhear, she said, "I saw you talking to Chris Talbot."

I shrugged. "We live on the same street, so now that he hasn't got a car, we ended up walking together."

"Do you think he did those burglaries?"

"I don't know enough to have an opinion. What do you think?"

She shook her head. "I don't think he's the breaking-and-entering type, and I also don't think he's good enough with a computer to hack into home security systems."

"Who do you think it was?"

"All the guys know about Chris' car, since he talks about it non-stop. Chris was supposed to be with his parents in Tallahassee, so someone could have figured they could use the car, do the robbery, and get it back before anyone knew it was gone. Nobody expected they'd run off the road and land in a lake."

"So who left Ricky in the car and ran?"

"No idea." She lowered her voice. "But I've started investigating." She touched a set of earbuds twined around the strap of her backpack. "A bunch of us walk to school together every day. Today, I pretended to listen to music while I really listened to Rooster and his buds ramble on about their pathetic lives."

"Why?"

She swatted my arm. "To find things out, genius."

"And what have you discovered, Nancy Drew?"

Ignoring my sarcasm, Birdy said, "Ricky and Chris had parted ways over the last few months."

"About what?"

"The guys don't know for sure." She glanced around to make sure no one was paying attention to us. "It wasn't a big, sock-you-in-the-eye thing, but Ricky started taking nasty jabs at Chris, saying he wasn't aggressive enough in football and he liked his car more than he liked his friends."

"What did Chris do about it?"

"He'd go all quiet, they said. Some of the guys think that's why he let Ricky drown, to pay him back for being mean."

"Ricky was aggressive toward Chris, yet they were supposedly robbing houses together on the weekends. That makes no sense."

"I know, but even Rooster noticed Ricky's attitude, and he doesn't notice much. Apparently, Ricky said once that Chris thought he was too good for his old buddies."

"Why would he think that?"

"Don't know. Other guys said they'd noticed it, but that's probably BS. If Ricky said something, the rest went along. They've been following his lead since kindergarten."

At that moment, Chris passed by. He ignored both of us, in fact, he ignored everyone, as he entered the school building, his head high and his eyes blank.

"Like Hester Prynne," Birdy said. "He faces his shame with pride and dignity." I frowned, trying to make the connection, and she elbowed me. "*The Scarlet Letter*, Loser!"

"Right," I said. "I always wondered who'd name their kid Hester."

Birdy put a hand on my arm, and it took me a second to refocus on what she was saying. "You should ask Chris what went wrong between him and Ricky."

Chris had talked like he knew Birdy. Now Birdy was all about Chris. Did they have a thing for each other? It was possible. It was also depressing.

"I told you about the feud between my guardian and the Talbots," I said. "We don't communicate much."

She sighed. "It would be nice to get his side of it, but—" The bell rang, signaling five minutes until the start of classes. "See you later."

The promise in those words made me happy for the rest of the morning.

At lunch time, when I left the serving line with my tray, Birdy was waiting for me. "There's a spot outside if you want to go there." Like we'd already talked about meeting for lunch, and she'd scouted out the best place.

Cool.

The spot was a bench, which made it tricky to keep from dropping my mac and cheese into my lap, but Birdy didn't notice. Stuffing fries and nuggets into her face as she talked, she told me about Denzel Washington's *Macbeth* movie ("Very cool"), dissecting a frog in biology ("Disgusting!"), and her experience with joining the soccer team the year before. "I had a killer side kick," she said as she chewed, "but I never got the hang of dribbling, so I sat the bench a lot."

"I don't think that matters if you liked being on the team."

"It was okay." Birdy shrugged. "I always have tons of stuff to do at home, and Dave kept asking what good soccer was ever going to do for me."

"Oh, well," I said teasingly. "They can take the girl out of soccer, but she'll always have that wicked sidekick."

Eventually, we got back to Ricky's death and Chris' guilt or innocence. I tried not to think about why Birdy defended Chris so strongly.

"I think this Home-Hack Gang had to be more than two kids," she said. "Ricky had the nerve to do the burglaries, and Chris might have gained the technical skill to hack the wi-fi. But I think there's probably someone else involved who figures out which houses to hit and sells–I guess the term is *fences*–what they steal."

"Yeah, Lorilee and I talked about that."

"Lorilee's your guardian?"

"Yeah. She's pretty smart."

Birdy finished her fries by wadding them together, dredging them in ketchup, and dropping them into her mouth. "Seems like the adult would have to know kids pretty well, like who needed money, who wanted money, who'd do the jobs and keep his mouth shut."

"A relative, maybe?"

"Or someone who works with kids, like here at school." I raised my brows, but she went on. "Teachers and coaches get to know kids."

The bell rang then, and we gathered up our stuff. "We should talk about this some more," I said, keeping my tone light. "Would it be okay if I came to your house tomorrow?"

She hesitated before answering. "I'll come to yours. I know where it is, because I visited Chris once." Hefting her book bag, she said, "Is ten okay? I have stuff to do in the afternoon."

"Sure." We went to our separate classes, but my mind was kind of a mess. Birdy was coming to my house, which was cool, but it felt like she was focused on Chris, which wasn't. Had she invited herself over because he lived next door? Because she might see him outside and get a chance to talk to him?

If Chris had rejected Birdy at some point in the past—He'd called her "different"—she might have been crushing on him for a long time. Did she think she'd get a second chance to be his girl now that he was friendless? In that case, I was a pawn in Birdy's game, allowing her to get next door to the guy she really liked.

The question bothered me so much that in science class, I asked Kacie if she knew Wendy Byrd.

"The girl with all the red hair? I talked with her a few times."

"I just wondered if she—" I couldn't make myself ask if she had a boyfriend, so I ended with a lame, "—might help me with an English paper."

"Well, she's really smart," Kacie said. "Not like her blockhead stepbrother Rooster."

The rest of the day passed in a haze, and the words "stepbrother Rooster" drowned out every teacher's carefully planned lesson. Birdy was Rooster Kalamaris' stepsister. She lived in the same house with a bully who hated my guts.

As soon as she saw me outside the school building, Birdy knew that I was angry. Her eyes met mine as I approached, and I felt my face turning redder with each step. Keeping my voice low so we wouldn't be overheard, I asked, "Why didn't you tell me about Rooster?"

After a long pause, Birdy said, "You don't know what it's like to have a completely dysfunctional family."

I laughed aloud, though it was a bitter rather than a happy sound. "Right. I don't know anything."

"I don't fit with my family," she said, twisting her fingers together. "I don't get their jokes, I don't share their views, I don't even remember the past the same way they do. Can you imagine what that's like?"

Looking out across the school campus, I answered her question. "I can. My dad hates the sight of me. He thinks I'm weak and soft, and he can't understand why I don't love guns and sports and cars and hunting camp. He never stopped trying to change me into the son he wanted, and it was killing me. So in June, I ran away from home. I made it this far and got a job with Dr. Ahuja at the shelter. I'd be broke and homeless right now if it weren't for Lorilee." I turned to her. "So yes, I know what it's like to have a messed-up family."

Birdy looked down at her hands as she told me her story. "My mom married Dave Kalamaris when I was eight. Rooster and I hated each other from Day One, but Mom said Dave was a good provider, so we were staying." She sniffed. "Now Mom's gone, and I'm stuck with them."

"I'm sorry."

Birdy shrugged. "It's okay. Dave pretty much ignores me. Rooster is … well, you can guess what Rooster's like."

"It can't be easy."

She ran a hand over her forehead. "I clean the house. I fix the meals. Dave hands me most of his paycheck every week so I can buy groceries and pay the bills." Her tone hardened. "They can't say I don't earn my keep." She touched the stack of books beside her on the seat, and I realized they served as a wall, keeping people out of Birdy's business.

"Do they treat you okay?"

She shrugged. "Dave's nice enough, but he isn't around much. Rooster's a jerk, but I know things that could get him in trouble, so he can't push me around."

"I bet he didn't like it when you told Gage the truth about the fight with Chris."

She smiled grimly. "I tell him all the time that I won't lie for him when he acts like an ass." She picked up her backpack. "You should go. You don't want to be late for work." Her tone was cool. As she walked away without once looking back, I felt confused. Was she giving me an excuse to back away? Was she letting me know that if I wanted it that way, we wouldn't speak again?

It was weird. I'd caught Birdy in a lie, yet she walked away from me with her spine tight, like she was the one who'd been offended.

"I think you made her mad," a voice said, and I turned to find Dylan, Ricky's cousin, standing behind me. She wore black leggings and a pink hoodie, and she tugged on a lock of her blond, kind of messy hair. Unlike Birdy, Dylan carried nothing with her as she left school, not even a purse.

I shrugged helplessly. "I didn't mean to."

"Are you two together?"

"I wish people would stop asking me that. I've known her for like, a few days."

Dylan smiled at me then, one of those full-on smiles that left no doubt that it was meant for me. She was pretty in a kind of fairy-tale way, tiny bones, big eyes, and a slightly pointed chin. "Maybe I'll see you around then."

"Maybe." I waved self-consciously and turned away. Where did I get the power to attract two cute girls in one week?

Chapter Seventeen

Lorilee

Birdy's name had come up a lot for a day or so, but when Jess learned her stepbrother was his arch enemy, he was confused, asking me why she wouldn't have told him that. I did my best to reassure him, though I wasn't sure myself. The simplest explanation was that she was ashamed of Rooster, since he sounded to me like an arrogant bully.

Unable to help Jess with his love life, I took the tablet to a sunny window and researched what was required to rob a smart house. I read anecdotes about the dire consequences when consumers used easy-to-break passwords, shared passwords with others, or typed in a password while someone was close enough to see and memorize it. The hacking part got pretty technical, and in the end, I decided to call an old friend at Family Services who was more computer savvy than I would ever be. After some catching-up chatter, I asked her if she thought a couple of untrained teenagers could hijack a smart home's systems.

"For some of them, that would be easy-peasy," my friend said. "In fact, if you want to hear it from the horse's mouth, you should talk to a girl we've got helping out here right now. She got caught hacking last spring, and rather than jail time, the judge had her work off her sentence by helping us protect our files from people like her." She chuckled. "She shows us stuff we wish we didn't have to know."

"Could I meet her if I came down there today?"

"Sure. She's ours every weekday from three to six." After a beat, my friend asked, "Why are you so interested, Lorilee?"

Unwilling to lie outright, I equivocated. "I have a young kid living with me for a while, and he's got a bug in his ear about hackers. I told him I'd talk to an expert."

After a bit more chatting and a promise to "do lunch" that would probably never materialize, I ended the call and went to change into clothing more presentable than grass-stained shorts and an oversized t-shirt.

For years after my accident, leaving home had been my least favorite thing to do. A combination of things, Jess' arrival, a corpse in my front yard, and the passage of time, had combined to nudge me back into the world a little. While I still didn't shop in stores, meet friends at restaurants, or attend social gatherings, I was willing to put on a bra, leave home, and make nice with humanity when it suited my purposes.

I entered the building where I'd worked for decades without the slightest sense of regret. I had liked my job, but I was done with it. It was nice to see a few familiar faces, and they all told me how wonderful I looked, but I felt the pity behind their smiles. *Poor Lorilee. She lost so much.* It's hard to relate to people who see you only as an example of how lucky they are to not be you.

Deb showed me to a desk in a corner, where a young woman sat tapping at a keyboard. She stopped, obviously reluctantly, when Deb introduced me, and her gaze kept returning to the screen. Her long, manicured nails moved constantly, as if her fingers were eager to get back to what they did so well.

Monique wore a Guns N' Roses t-shirt, shorts, and high-top tennis shoes. Her long, dark hair was parted in the center and left loose. She wore huge hoop earrings, oversized, amber-lensed glasses, and an expression that said she wished I'd go away. Being forced to work for the state was no doubt irritating, but now her boss was making her answer questions from an old woman she'd never met.

I flattered her a little, telling her I needed expert help. Monique responded slightly, flashing me a brief smile. Getting down to business so she wouldn't feel I was wasting her time, I asked her to help me understand how someone around her age might turn off a sophisticated home security system.

Monique gave me a knowing look. "You're related to that kid that robbed houses and then let his buddy drown."

"Not related, but he's my neighbor."

Monique's plump lips pressed together. "Well, first I gotta say that it blows, leaving a friend to die."

"What if he didn't do it?"

"How would you know?" Her tone was snotty and she rocked her head in a way that signaled disrespect.

I kept my smile in place. "I don't know. But the kid doesn't seem like the type who'd leave anyone to die, much less a friend." Waving a hand as if pushing that argument aside, I went on, "It's hard to say what a person will do in a given situation. Fear makes people do strange things. So I'd like to set aside the type of person he is and consider whether a kid of seventeen is capable of planning and carrying out these crimes." I leaned toward her. "That's why I came to you."

"Bet."

That confused me, but I soon understood that Monique spoke a language I had no acquaintance with. I'd brought along a pad and pencil, so I made notes, hoping Jess could translate the teen-speak into normal English. Like Jess' oddly-spelled texts, Monique's slang usually turned out to be a short version of a word or phrase we all understand. *Bet* meant "for sure," as in, "You can bet on it."

Unaware that she'd confused me, Monique went on. "People think their homes are safe because they buy smart devices, but then they do dumb stuff like leave the default password in place or use 'password 1234.' Pathetic."

"I read a little about it, so I know passwords can be hacked if they're repetitive or predictable."

She nodded. "Hackers can choose some boujee (fancy) place and try passwords until they hack into the router. The router controls the wi-fi, so everything is connected. It used to take time, but now there are ways to speed the process up. If the password is easy, it takes about two minutes."

"Amazing."

"A lot of adults got no clue. The kid who mows your lawn could be sniffing your network and you'd never even know it. Once he's in, he can set up what's called a 'man in the middle' attack. That means everything you do online goes through his site before it goes on to wherever you mean it to. He gets your passwords, your account numbers—everything. It's bussin'." (That meant really good ... if committing cybercrime is a good thing.)

"Can't the police catch people doing these things?"

"They try, but we—I mean, the hackers—get better every day." Monique pushed her hair back from her face. "I was always careful to clear my logs every time, and I'd divert my trail through some foreign country, so it was hard to follow."

That confused me, but I got the gist. "You were careful."

"Right. If you're sloppy ..." Monique had a story, and she told it with relish. "This friend of mine was a simp (guy trying to impress a girl) who got all thirsty (eager for attention) for this Deanna chick. He takes her out one night, drives to the parking lot of a chain store, and hacks their system. He was showin' out, you know?" She rolled her eyes. "He took way too many shortcuts, and now he's doing time. And that girl Deanna? She won't even take his calls."

"How did you get caught?"

Her mouth turned down. "I ran into a real hard-nosed type. I never thought he'd get so salty (upset) about what I did, but I learned a lesson: If you make somebody mad enough, they really come after you."

"What did you do?"

"Not tryin' to flex (flaunt one's accomplishments), but girl, I'm good. I played around with hacking, but I didn't do anything serious until I had a little problem with geometry class. The teacher failed me, and I needed it to graduate, you get me?"

Remembering Jess' mention of a friend who'd changed his absences on his school's computers, I said, "You went into the system to change the grade."

"Nothin' to it." Monique's right brow rose. "The system at my high school was a joke, and once I fixed my own problem, I started making good money changing grades or absences for other students. I figured I'd keep that up when I got to college, but it was different there." She tapped an air-brushed fingernail on the table between us. "I couldn't hack my way into their system. If I was going to keep my little student-helper business going, I had to get into the tech's office and access his computer."

"Because..."

"Because even somebody with a tight system gets lazy in his own office. Who wants to sign out and sign in all the time to every site? Who wants to wait for that authentication code to show up on your phone and then type it in every time?" Monique leaned toward me, forgetting for a moment that I was one of the clueless old people she despised. "In his office, where a guy feels comfortable, he tends to let the computer remember everything. He doesn't close the programs he uses all the time. He lets the computer remember his passwords for the sites he uses a lot." She gave me an arch look. "The problem is that the computer doesn't know who's booting it up."

"So you needed to get into the records office."

"Yeah. I figured once a week would be good. I typed up a letter, supposedly from the registrar, that said he'd hired me—well, I posed as a guy named Mark Martin— to 'update and monitor the health' of his computer. The note said I was to do the work at night, so it didn't interrupt the flow of data during the school day. I found the registrar's signature online and copied and pasted it onto the note. Then, late at night, when there was only a janitor around, I showed up dressed as Mark Martin, flashed a friend's old fake ID, and gave him the letter." She sat back, pleased with herself. "He let me into the office and, as I'd figured, it was a piece of cake from there. The main entry code was written on his desk blotter. All his passwords were 'saved to this device.' No thumbprint required to get into anything. That first night, I fixed my math grade and gave my roommate a *B* in Ancient History II. Soon I was making good money, changing grades, sometimes even giving people credit for taking a class they never stepped foot in."

"It didn't last."

"It did not." Her mouth twisted. "One week I had to go in on a different night, and the janitor on duty was the suspicious type. After I left, he wrote a note and left it on the registrar's desk. He got all extra (dramatic) and called in the cops, who found one of my hairs on the floor by the desk." She patted her hair resentfully. "I wore a cap as part of my Mark Martin disguise, but I took it off while I was working because it made my head sweat."

"And that single hair betrayed you?"

"Sure did." Monique sounded disgusted. "Can you believe they analyzed the DNA? I was in the system because I did an ancestry search last year." She ran her tongue over her teeth. "Anyway, they made it sound like I committed treason. The registrar insisted I wouldn't have been satisfied with changing grades for long, and that eventually I'd have started stealing school funds." She made the phrases ring with sarcasm. "It was a total cap (lie), but here I am, on probation and giving tech advice to little old ladies."

"And I appreciate your help." Thanks to Gunter's influence, I was able to keep every bit of sarcasm out of my voice.

Monique returned to my original question. "So the answer is yes. Your teenagers could have done exactly what the cops think they did. Hackers learn by doing, so they probably taught themselves."

"Incredible."

Monique tilted her head. "Now, if it was me, I wouldn't even have gone inside. I'd have sat in my car in the driveway and emptied their bank accounts." She folded her arms on the table. "Much more efficient."

Having worked with kids for decades, I had an idea about that. "But teens, especially boys, in my experience, crave excitement. Taking chances, exploring someone else's home, stealing what they wanted, it was all part of the kick."

"Too bad only one of them lived through it." Monique's brown eyes flashed angrily. "I still think your neighbor deserves to be in jail for letting his friend drown."

"I'm not sure he was anywhere near that lake," I told her, "but I don't have a way to prove that yet."

Chapter Eighteen

Jess

Doc Ahuja texted to say that Green's family had been located, so I went home to get the cat before heading to work Friday afternoon. As I chased him down and put him in the carrier (How do cats always know when you plan to take them somewhere?) I debated mentioning Birdy's upcoming visit to Lorilee. We'd never discussed dating, so I wasn't sure how she'd feel about me inviting a girl over. Would she get mad? Would she tease me about having a girlfriend?

I wasn't even sure Birdy would show. She'd sounded funny when she offered to come, like she didn't really want to. In the end, I decided to say nothing and let the visit happen if it happened. Afterward I could be casual about it, like, "Oh, she said she might stop by, but it wasn't for sure."

Lorilee gave Green a few goodbye pets and told him he'd been a good cat. Leaving the house, I saw Nasty Greg's head peeking over the fence top. He held binoculars he'd trained on the house, so he didn't see me coming. I went around the fence and saw that he was standing on an overturned trash can. From his vantage point, he could look into the guest bedroom, where makeshift sleeping boxes, butter-tub food dishes, garbage-bag-and-cardboard litter pans, and toys betrayed the presence of multiple cats, obviously more than the eight we were allowed.

"Get down from there," I ordered.

Greg jumped when I spoke, but he soon recovered his snotty attitude. "I'm on my own property, and I ain't hurting you."

He was right, and there was no sense in arguing. Giving him a dirty look, I went on. He didn't notice; he was already back to watching cats come and go.

How did Chris tolerate his irritating little brother? Having never had siblings, I didn't know much about ten-year-old boys, but Greg seemed delighted to be able to make trouble. I tried to picture dinner at the Talbot home: Mitzi blathering on, Chris saying little, Greg making smart-aleck comments, and the dad ignoring them all. Even with our current overload of cats, Lorilee and I had a lot more fun than that.

Chapter Nineteen

Lorilee

Green was on his way home. As for the others, we were becoming used to their eccentricities. Blue, the anxious cat who had at first refused to use a litter box, calmed down when Jess took her basket, litter tray, and food dishes into his room. "She needs a quiet space," he said, and he was right. When not forced to socialize with the others, Blue became a different, calmer cat.

Indigo and Yellow still tore through the house like stampeding wildebeests. Violet came out from under the bed once in a while, but each time she did, she felt the need to vocalize her fears, loudly and constantly. I spent my days refereeing fights between the Professor and Red and saving what furniture I could from Orange's compulsive climbing and shredding. I laid sheets over the upholstered furniture, so the house looked like a set for a film about a haunted mansion.

With extra cats to care for and clean up after, I hadn't worked in the yard much lately, and it showed. Late Friday afternoon, I left the noise and chaos inside and stole a few minutes to finish cleaning up the remaining storm debris.

In order to get pickup, we were required to bundle large branches and set them out by the road. Leaves, fronds, and smaller bits went into a large brown bin that was picked up separately from the household garbage. Jess usually did the heavy lifting, since my bad hip rebelled at such tasks, but he'd been so busy lately, juggling school, work, and our ubiquitous boarders, that I hated to ask him to do one more chore. I told myself I could get the yard waste to the road if I took it slow and rested often.

Filling the wheelbarrow with debris, I tested the weight of it and glared resentfully, rubbing the hip that already ached from the effort. Tottering like a punch-drunk boxer, I pushed the barrow out to the street, where I'd already set the trash bin. I stood looking from one to the other when

I heard someone say, "Let me help." Turning, I saw Chris hurrying toward me. "Want this in there?"

"That would be great." As I stood by, envious, he lifted the whole wheelbarrow and dumped it into the bin. "Not in school this afternoon?"

"Mental health break." He gave me a rueful grin. "I made it to lunch time. Then I was ready to be out of there."

After picking up a few bits that had fallen onto the ground, Chris maneuvered the barrow back to my gateway, where he stopped, tacitly acknowledging that he wasn't allowed on my property. I'm not sure whether it was more gratitude or curiosity, but I asked, "Would you like to try the apple tarts I made this morning?" When he looked doubtful, I said, "I won't tell anyone you came over if you don't."

He leaned back to peer at his house before answering. "Yeah. That would be nice."

Soon we were in my kitchen. As I got us each a tart, Special Ed came in and sat down, tilting his head at the newcomer. "What would you like to drink?"

"Water, please. I don't like sugary stuff, and I don't think much of artificial sweeteners either."

"I wish you'd tell Jess that," I said. "His favorite drink is some kind of manufactured toxin."

"He's a good dude though."

"That's very true." I took a sip. "He told me how you stood up for him at school."

Apparently embarrassed by that, Chris avoided responding by pointing to Callie, who'd come into the kitchen and sat down next to Ed. "Which cats are these?"

"That's Ed, and that's Caledonia—Callie."

Mayson and May showed up, their noses raised slightly as they examined our guest. Yellow and Indigo rolled by the doorway, swatting at a ball and sliding on their backsides. Chris seemed a little overwhelmed, so I offered some assurance. "Most of them won't bother you. Callie does like men, so she might try to jump onto your lap."

He seemed watchful but not particularly negative. "I've never been around cats. My little brother's allergic, and Mom—" He stopped, unsure how to finish.

"—thinks cats are evil." Two more boarder cats, Orange and Red, sauntered by, and it occurred to me that if the kid counted, he'd easily come up with more heads than eight.

He didn't seem to be counting. "It's my grandmother's fault. She had all these old superstitions she used to insist were true. Cats will suck a baby's breath away. If you look a cat in the eye, it will take your soul. Your cat will eat you if you die."

I snickered. "If there's no other food source, that last one is probably true. First and foremost, cats are survivors."

"Makes sense to me. Anyway, Mom never got over all that. She thinks cats are sneaky and scary."

Bruiser wandered in and took a seat in the doorway. Noting his extra toes, crooked tail, and lopped off ear tip, Chris gave me a look of amusement. "Yes," I said agreeably. "Each of my cats is quite individual."

Callie moved a few steps closer to Chris' chair and I bent to pick her up and set her on my lap. If Greg really was allergic, it wouldn't do for Chris to go home covered in cat hair.

I was tempted to ask how the investigation into Ricky Fulmer's death was going, but I guessed Chris was tired of thinking about that. Instead I asked, "Why did you speak up for Jess when that boy at school harassed him?"

Taking a bite of tart, he chewed for a while. "I'm not sure."

"Well, why do you think you might have done it?"

He ate the rest of the tart and took a sip of water before he answered. "We've only lived here for two years, so I remember how it felt that first week, being the new kid. Our first hour teacher asked Birdy to show me around, and she was great, but the guys pretty much ignored me until I joined the football team."

"Teams are great for that."

"But guys like Jess shouldn't get harassed because they don't play football or act in school plays or join the robotics club."

"It's too bad some of your friends don't share your attitude."

"Lately I feel like ... I don't know. The guys aren't as much fun as I used to think they were."

"Maybe you grew up." I might have added, *and they didn't.*

Chris' face reddened. "Our neighbor Mr. Fusilli had a talk with me a while back. He's a good dude."

I'd become aware that "good dude" was Chris' highest compliment. "About the drinking?"

"Yeah. He said I could hide in a beer bottle, like my dad does, or I could choose to be different."

"Fusilli said that to you?"

"Just like that." Chris smiled grimly. "Some people think kids don't know they've got a functioning alcoholic for a parent, but trust me, we do."

That was my experience after working with kids in the system. They coped with bad parenting, they even accepted it, but they usually knew it wasn't right. "How did your friends react when you stopped partying with them?"

He sniffed. "They were all like, 'So you think you're better than us?' I said no, but it made things different." Taking another drink, he said, "Now they're sure I left Ricky in that lake." He met my gaze. "I wasn't there, Ms. Riley."

"Did Ricky steal your car?"

"I think so."

"And did he rob that house?"

An odd expression formed on his face. "Probably."

"Who would have been driving?"

"I don't know," Chris said, "but it would have been me if I'd said yes."

"To the work he offered you a few months ago."

"Yeah. When school started this fall, Rick had this expensive smartwatch and a new phone with all the extras." I pushed the plate in his direction, and Chris took a second tart. "His mom is a waitress. She can't afford to buy him stuff like that."

"Did you ever get a hint as to who he's working with, or for?"

There was no answer for a while. Chris ate the tart, finished the glass of water, and then rose and set his plate and glass in the sink. "I should go. Thanks for the snack, Ms. Riley. It was really good."

I rose too. "Chris—" What to say? The kid was suffering. He knew something about Ricky's death that he wouldn't—maybe couldn't—tell. "Come by again if you'd like to talk." I raised a finger. "But remember, keep the invitation between us."

Chapter Twenty

Jess

Science class was almost pleasant for once, since Rooster was absent. Our experiments were coming along well, and Kacie was meticulous about documenting everything we learned. It looked like the project would be a success, and even Erin was interested to learn the difference between the hype and the truth in terms of energy drinks. I was unhappy to learn that my favorite, Liquid Breeze, was loaded with sugar and not much else. Maybe Lorilee was right, and I should drink more water.

"I saw you with that Wendy Byrd." Erin, who had never spoken directly to me before, leaned closer. "Are you two together?" While I tried to come up with a response that gave no information and no offense, Erin added, "It's just that Ricky Fulmer used to say bad stuff about her, so you might want to be careful."

I should have stopped myself, but I couldn't. "What did he say?"

Kacie gave Erin a look. "Shut up." To me she said, "It isn't worth repeating."

"He didn't say anything specific," Erin said, but an added sparkle in her eyes hinted she was savoring my distress. "He always called her Rooster's 'stepsister with benefits.'"

"Hey, Erin," Kacie said, "can you get us some more test tubes from the closet?" When Erin rose and left the table, Kacie said, "Listen. Erin is the original mean girl, so don't say anything about Birdy to her or around her. If you do, she'll tell the whole world, and she'll put her own spin on it to make you sound bad."

I was trying to swallow my shock at Erin's statement. "It isn't true," I told Kacie. "Birdy can't stand Rooster."

"She couldn't stand Ricky either." Raising her brows meaningfully, Kacie added, "I think that was the whole problem."

Gathering my courage, I asked, "What about Birdy and Chris Talbot? Were they ever a thing?"

Kacie frowned. "Not that I remember, but I don't keep track of Birdy's love life." With a grin she added, "If I did, would you be on the list?"

I liked Kacie and recognized that she was teasing, so I grinned back at her. "No idea," I said. "Ask me again next week."

Birdy had to go to the pharmacy after school, so we took a new route, a little out of my direct path to work, but not bad. I had dismissed Erin's nasty insinuation as mean-girl garbage, like Kacie recommended. We talked about stuff, the kind of natural conversation I enjoyed with her, and I told myself not to be insecure and paranoid. Birdy must like being with me, or she wouldn't hang with me every day.

As we came down Coral Street, a man came out of the side door of a convenience store, carrying a bag of trash. Crossing the parking lot, he tossed the bag into a trash bin set in a walled-off corner.

"Hey," I said to Birdy. "That's the guy who went after Chris in the alley."

"Are you sure?" When I nodded, she said, "Stu owns that place. I don't go in there much, but Rooster and the guys do."

The small, squat store had signs in every window, advertising a variety of offerings, including "homemade" pizza, ice cream, cigarettes, and lottery tickets. It didn't look like a place for planning midnight crimes, but then again, I wasn't an expert on the subject.

Chapter Twenty-One

Lorilee

It isn't easy to chase down a cop and pick his brain. I couldn't waylay Deputy Brilli while he waited at the local speed trap, or drop in at the sheriff's office and invite myself to a cup of overdone coffee. Even if I had known where I might find him, he'd be unwilling to share what he knew with a private citizen. And if his half-brother Detective Law happened to see us chatting, he'd be beyond unhappy. My best bet, I decided, was to attend a public event where a detective wasn't likely to be in attendance but a deputy would be, to provide security. In Florida there are a lot of those, and I found two listed online that weekend. The county was hosting a Fun Run on Saturday, and the nearby town of Collins had a Pride Parade scheduled. Given the option, I guessed Brilli would choose the former, since races seldom attract controversy. I'd go there first.

He was indeed at the Fun Run, held to raise money for children with cancer. I found him posted at the entry beside his car, arms folded across his chest as he watched the runners sign in.

"Deputy Brilli, good morning."

He frowned when he saw it was me, but I was ready. Holding out the bag, I carried, I said, "Macaroons."

The frown disappeared ... almost. Taking the bag, he said, "What are you doing here, Ms. Riley?"

I chuckled. "Well, I don't run, so you know it's not for the race."

"If you're worried about your young man, the Talbot boy told us his mother was 'mistaken' about Jess showing interest in his car." He made air quotes around the word to show what he thought of Mitzi's fabrication.

"I wondered what you've learned about those burglaries."

Brilli's expression turned exasperated. "Ms. Riley, you know I can't—"

"You don't have to tell state secrets. I only want to know if you still think Chris is guilty."

He sighed. "*I* do, but we're no closer to proving it."

"It seems a stretch to me to believe that two teens from Linville planned a bunch of home invasions in Tampa's fancier neighborhoods, hacked the protection devices with their cyber-smarts, and disposed of the stolen property, all while attending high school and playing football on Friday nights."

Another sigh. "You could be right. Jim thinks there's a third person involved."

"Any idea who it might be?"

Brilli sniffed. "If I had one, I couldn't tell you about it."

"It would have to be someone the boys knew well."

Brilli said nothing.

"Possibly a person at the school, such as a teacher or a coach."

Brilli said nothing.

"Or it could be a relative."

Silence.

"Mitzi has family in the area." His eyes flicked toward me, interested, but he still said nothing. "I don't think they're close, though. She never talks about them."

Raised voices at the starting line caught Brilli's attention. "Gotta go, Ms. R. Thanks for the cookies." Setting them on the seat of his cruiser, he went off to settle a disagreement about proper attire.

When I got home, Jess was sitting on the patio with a girl. As I got out of the car and approached, he rose from his chair, looking nervous. "Lorilee, this is Birdy, the one who got me out of detention the other day."

"Hello, Birdy. I think we both owe you thanks, since Jess hates detention and I hate injustice."

"Me too," Birdy said. "That's why I had to say something." At first sight, she reminded me of the girl I'd once been, unable, perhaps unwilling, to learn the complicated beauty regimens of her contemporaries. She wore no makeup, her brows were natural, and her reddish hair was pulled back in a no-nonsense, slightly bushy ponytail. The set of her chin hinted that she'd be judged by her own standards, not anyone else's.

A plate of macaroons sat on the table between them, and they each had a glass of the purple stuff Jess drinks.

"Where'd you go?" he asked.

"I tracked down our friend Brilli and asked him a few questions."

Jess nodded at Birdy. "We were talking about the mess Chris is in. Birdy doesn't think he'd do what they say he did."

"You know Chris?" I asked the girl.

"A little." She shrugged lightly. "He's not a Neanderthal, like most of his friends."

"Lorilee agrees with you, Birdy," Jess said. "She's not sure Chris did anything wrong, and she thinks there's an adult behind this gang."

The girl looked at me questioningly. "You think someone sends them out to steal?"

I raised my brows, lowered my voice, and did a bad British accent. 'Run along, my dears, and don't come back empty handed.'"

Birdy chuckled. "You do a pretty good Fagin impression."

"Who?" Jess asked.

Birdy turned to him, her eyes wide. "You've never seen *Oliver!*?"

Jess frowned. "Maybe. Some of it. A long time ago." In a defensive tone, he finished, "I never saw much sense in movies where people break into song and dance in perfect step. That doesn't happen in real life."

Birdy rolled her eyes at me as if to say, *He doesn't get it.* Aloud she said, "My mom loved musicals, so I've got all the old ones practically memorized."

I noted the past tense. "Your mom died?"

"Yes."

"I'm sorry."

Perhaps to avoid further discussion of a painful topic, Birdy said, "If there is a Fagin, he's responsible for Ricky's death, whether he was driving that car or sitting at home waiting for them to bring him the loot."

"Yes," I said. "I believe a death during the commission of a crime makes everyone involved liable."

"Do you think Fagin could be somebody at school, like a teacher or a coach?" The girl's eyes lit with interest, and I sensed a problem arising. It was one thing for Jess and me to discuss a crime and maybe poke around a little, but involving another person, especially one neither of us knew very well, was not a good idea.

I sensed a problem; Jess saw an opportunity. "Birdy knows everyone," he said. "She could talk to people and then we could—"

"It's an active police investigation," I interrupted. "We wouldn't want Detective Law to think we're interfering with his case." I didn't add "again," but I gave Jess a look that hinted at it. Then I changed the subject. "Has Birdy met the cats?"

He blushed. "Um, no. We didn't go inside. I mean I did, to get the food and stuff, but—" The sentence trailed away as his face got even redder.

"Well then, Birdy, come inside and meet the gang," I invited. "If you don't run away screaming, you're welcome back anytime."

After Birdy met everyone from Callie to Poor Kitty, she said she had to get home and rode off on a bicycle that had seen better days. When she was gone, Jess said, "You really don't want to know who at the school might be your Fagin guy?"

"We might … observe and … discuss possibilities," I said, "but since we're not in any way official, it's best to keep it between us."

He seemed offended. "Birdy wouldn't tell anyone."

"I'm sure she wouldn't, but we don't want to get her in trouble with Detective Law, do we?"

"No way."

"And you certainly don't want to put your new friend in danger."

He shook his head.

"Then let's keep any investigation we conduct to ourselves."

"Okay." Jess seemed unsure how to express his next concern. "I hope it's all right that Birdy came over."

I waved his words away. "This is your home, Jess. You have the right to invite guests and offer them whatever we've got for refreshments."

He nodded. "I didn't think it was right for us to be inside … you know … alone."

Though I appreciated that, I wasn't sure how to respond. Behavioral standards are different than they were when I was seventeen, and while I didn't want to seem prudish, I wasn't about to assure him that I'd be okay with them having sex in my second spare bedroom. In the end, I said only, "Birdy seems nice."

"She is."

I left it at that. Though the girl seemed intelligent and "together," teens are often good at presenting whatever persona fits an adult's expectations. Was Birdy trustworthy? If she wasn't, I doubted Jess could see it. Not with all that first-love brightness shining in his eyes.

Chapter Twenty-Two

Jess

Dr. Ahuja and I returned to Fort Myers on Sunday, this time to help a local vet care for the animals in her clinic. While the doc did surgeries, mended breaks, and bandaged cuts, I helped the staff bathe animals rescued from areas where the floods had receded. The dogs, cats, and one ferret that searchers had found were dirty and malnourished, and they all had a lost look in their eyes that broke my heart.

"We never know what they've been into," a staffer told me, "but it's probably not good for them, so we hose 'em down, first thing."

Some animals smelled of sewage, like the cat Bruiser had brought home. Others had waded or swum through water contaminated by garbage or chemicals. As the animals were brought in, we used rags, brushes, and dish soap to clean them thoroughly. They were surprisingly accepting, though every single dog had to do the shake-it-off thing when their bath was done, getting everyone in the vicinity wet.

The work felt good, and we laughed at the animals' antics. Still, it was sobering to hear the stories told by the staff. Some were living in motels or with friends. One woman was sleeping at the office, since she had no other place to stay. A guy named Brian said his grandfather had died of heart failure when they couldn't get him to a hospital. Another guy, Joe, had suffered for days, unsure if his sister was dead or alive, before finally hearing from her. Still, they were cheerful with each other and gentle with their charges.

As we worked, a figure appeared in the open back door. I looked up to see a kid of about seven peering in at us.

Joe was toweling off a pit bull, but he called, "Can we help you, bud?"

"My dog, Digger. I haven't been able to find him since the storm."

"Did he run away?"

The kid bit his bottom lip. "He was in the garage, and a tree fell on it. When we got out there, Digger was gone."

The guy next to me shook his head. "Poor critter ran scared and got lost."

"Tell us what Digger looks like," Joe said.

"He's a Lab." The kid paused. "We call him Digger, because he's always making holes in the yard."

"Black or golden?"

"Black. He's not chipped, but he's got a green collar."

Joe nodded. "Wait right there and I'll go have a look."

A woman appeared behind the kid. "Any luck, Sam?"

"The man's gonna check, Mom."

The woman put her hands on her son's shoulders. Though she smiled at us, I saw sadness in her eyes. "You're our sixth stop. Lots of lost dogs. No Digger."

The kid countered his mom's negativity with hopefulness. "Labs are really good swimmers," he said firmly.

The woman's lips pressed together, and she lifted a hand to wipe at her eyes. "There was blood on the garage floor," she said. "We don't know how bad—"

She was interrupted by a shout from Sam as he looked past us into the depths of the kennel. I turned to see Joe being dragged forward by an excited dog with a bandaged front shoulder.

Joe released the leash, and the dog rushed to meet the boy, making yips of joy as he almost knocked the kid down. "Digger!" Sam said, burying his face in his friend's coat. "Digger, Digger, Digger."

I lowered my eyes to hide a few tears, so I didn't see, but I'd guess there wasn't a dry eye in the place.

Chapter Twenty-Three

Lorilee

One advantage to having the recovering Poor Kitty in the house was that Bruiser had suspended his forays outside. He seemed to feel responsible for her welfare and was never far from her side. Though it was cute to watch, I dreaded the day when her owners came to claim her. Bruiser would never understand that the little cat belonged somewhere else.

Sunday was perfect for being outside, mid-seventies with warm but not blazing sunlight, so I went to work on my recently neglected flower beds. Using my little garden scooter, I moved from bed to bed, scraping weeds away with a forked trowel. I was thinking of absolutely nothing but the next weed, which is one of the best things there is about gardening.

"Ms. Riley?" I looked up to see Chris standing near the low stone wall that fronted my property.

"Good morning, Chris. Beautiful day."

He looked around as if he hadn't noticed. His eyes were rimmed with red, his posture tense as he hovered near my wall. Since it was far too early for anyone in his family to be up and around on a weekend, I guessed he'd been unable to sleep. "I'm sorry to always be bothering you—"

"Don't be silly," I interrupted. "You're no bother at all." Standing, I brushed my hands on my shorts. "Have you had anything to eat? I'm sure I could find a little something for us."

He was over the wall in a heartbeat. "Thanks," he said. "Whatever you've got would be great." As he followed me inside, Chris said, "I can't decide where I want to be these days. I don't want to be out with people, but when I'm alone my mind just goes over and over everything that's bad. I can't say anything about it to Mom, because she cries."

"Well, I'm sorry I can't be any real help," I told him, "but you're always welcome to come over here and sit for a while."

When we came in the kitchen door, Eddie and May were there. Eddie came forward to rub against Chris' pant leg, and somewhat tentatively, the kid leaned down to pet him. That brought Mayson, who wasn't about to miss out on any available affection, and Orange, who for once wasn't hanging from the draperies. As I pointed Chris to a chair and got out some cookies for a snack, Yellow and Indigo scampered by the doorway in full race mode. A moment later, Poor Kitty, who had started to move around more, came along. Bruiser was there, acting as her chaperone, and not to be left out of anything interesting, Callie followed. If anyone was counting, she made nine.

Since it was obvious, I confessed. "I'm boarding some cats left homeless by the hurricane," I said. "They aren't permanent, but right now, the place is a zoo."

"That's really nice of you," Chris said. "From what I saw on the news, it's bad down south."

"That's where Jess is today. He and the vet went to Fort Myers to help with caring for animals."

Leaning back in his chair, Chris peered into the living room. "There sure are a lot of them. How do you keep track?"

I introduced each cat, explaining the collars that allowed us to identify the non-permanent residents by color. "Good idea," he said approvingly.

Surprisingly, since it wasn't meal time, the Professor strolled into the kitchen and plopped down beside Chris' chair.

"You must be someone special," I said. "Professor Higgins generally dislikes people. He doesn't approve of being petted, picked up, or otherwise bothered, so you should simply enjoy the fact that he found you interesting enough to examine up close."

"A no-fuss pet," Chris said to the cat. "You sound like my kind of guy."

I could swear the Professor nodded. Cats sense emotion, and I wondered if the old cat realized Chris needed a little peace in his life. While he couldn't relax his standards and actually cuddle with a human, it seemed he was lending what comfort he could to our stressed, sad visitor.

Sitting down opposite Chris, I got right to the matter that I thought was upsetting him. "You've been holding something back, something you know that you haven't told anyone yet. If I promise not to pass it on, would you tell me? We could talk it out together."

He pressed his lips together for a moment, as if trying to force them to remain closed. Then he kind of collapsed. "I might know who Ricky was working for."

"Fagin," I breathed, and Chris looked at me in confusion.

"That's not his name."

"No, of course not. Who is it?"

"Do you know about Stu's?"

"What's that?"

"It's a convenience store near the school. There's groceries and stuff, but Stu has a few booths in one corner. Most places don't like kids hanging around all the time, but Stu likes us there. He's all about his glory days on the Linville High football team."

"Stu's." I filed it away, meaning to ask Jess about it.

"Last spring, I noticed that Ricky and Stu had gotten real close. When we'd all go there for pizza, the two of them would go off in a corner and talk, like they didn't want the rest of us to hear."

"Did you say anything to Ricky about it?"

"What would I say? 'Hey, I think you're doing illegal stuff and I wish you'd stop?'"

"Good point."

"On the day he died, Ricky called me. He said his car wouldn't start, and he needed me to drive him somewhere. I said I was sick, which I was, but he kept saying I had to help him out. He got all mad, and I finally said, 'Dude, you've been kind of a jerk to me lately. Call your buddy Stu and ask him to take you.'" Chris frowned as he finished. "Ricky said something odd. He said, 'That's not Stu's job.'"

"Then Stu was part of the crimes but not an active part?"

"That's how I took it." Chris set his plate in the sink and leaned against the countertop. "I think Ricky and some other kid were supposed to do the robbery. The other kid hasn't got a car. When Ricky's car wouldn't start, they took mine, figuring they'd get it back before anyone knew it was missing."

"This other person was driving when the car went off the bridge."

Chris nodded. "And because the police think it was me, they aren't looking for anyone else."

Rising, I set my own plate in the sink and then sat back down. "You're sure it couldn't have been Stu?"

"He's at the store until midnight on Saturdays. Plus, Stu's got a nice, new pickup, so they wouldn't have needed to take my car."

"But after Ricky died, Stu threatened you in the alley by the post office."

"Yeah. He said I should keep my mouth shut about what I know. I told him that would be easy, since I don't know anything."

"I see."

Though I'd learned it in disjointed segments, the story held together logically. Chris had no reason to come to my home and lie to me, at least, not one I could discern.

That didn't mean I could help. I had no power to erase the suspicions of the police. I couldn't convince members of the media and the community that he was innocent. All I could do was be a sounding board whenever a bit of the information he'd kept to himself boiled out of him.

"You're sure you have no idea who else is involved in the robberies?"

He shook his head. "When Ricky tried to ..."

"Recruit you," I supplied.

"I guess that's the word. He mentioned a 'boss' who'd have to check me out, but he said I could do it right after school and still make football practice. The way Ricky bragged about how smart the boss was, it didn't sound like Stu."

"So there's another adult involved?"

"I guess so. Like I said, I don't *know*. It's just what I'm putting together from thinking about this twenty-four-seven."

"Okay." I rose from my chair. "I'll try to get Detective Law to investigate this Stu person, and I'll do it without implicating you."

That cheered him a little. "Yeah, Mom said you're his friend."

"Not exactly, but he knows I'm honest." I smiled. "He might also say I'm nosy, but in this case, that might be a good thing."

Chris seemed relieved to have shared his secret. "Don't let anyone know it was me who told. I'd hate to get my house firebombed or something."

Showing him to the door, I promised, "I'll be discreet."

Chapter Twenty-Four

Jess

When Doc and I returned to Purr-fect Pets Sunday afternoon, there was a voicemail from the family of one of our boarders. They were living in temporary housing and saw no way they'd be able to care for a pet in the future. The cat Lorilee and I called Yellow was released for adoption.

I was sad to hear of the people's misfortune and sad that Yellow had no home. We'd do our best to place him, but good homes were hard to find. At least at our house, Yellow had Indigo. The two of them running around at all hours was irritating sometimes, but they were happy together. I'd added bells to their yarn collars to warn the other cats, Lorilee, me, and any stray anole lizards that they were around.

At home, Lorilee surprised me by confessing that Chris Talbot had visited, not once, but three times so far. "I wasn't trying to keep secrets from you," she said apologetically after telling me what he'd confided. "He shows up, asks a question or tells me some bit of information, and goes away again. I think he feels he has no one he can talk to."

"Shouldn't he be telling Detective Law about this Stu guy?"

"I suggested it, but Chris is correct. What can he offer as proof?"

"I saw the man push Chris against a wall in that alley."

"But you don't know why. Chris might claim it was about the burglaries, but the man could contend it was something else entirely. He said, he said."

"Yeah."

"This boss Ricky spoke of interests me. If we could identify him, or at least narrow down the possibilities, I could contact Detective Law and ask him to check out Stu and whoever."

"Where would we even start? It could be anyone."

"I think the school is the place to start. Chris said Ricky claimed he could meet the boss between the time school got out and football practice."

"You think one of our teachers is running a burglary ring."

Lorilee shrugged. "Teachers know the students, and they often have a lot of influence over them." She raised her brows. "How might we go about finding a staff member who's recruiting young criminals?"

"I guess I'd look for a teacher who's a little too close to the students."

"Such as?"

I thought about it. "Well, Birdy gripes that her English teacher is popular with the boys. She always has a bunch of them standing around her desk, so Birdy can't get to her to ask a question." After a few seconds, I said, "The guy that runs the computer lab would know about hacking." A little more thought brought two more possibilities. "I hear there's a janitor who sells pot to students. And everybody jokes that the assistant football coach is all palsy with the guys, hanging with them and stuff. They think he's desperate to feel like a kid again, but he could be up to something else."

"You're very observant."

I grinned. "If you don't talk, you get a lot more chances to listen."

"Do you think you could arrange to meet these people? I'd like your impression of how honest they are."

I frowned. "I guess I could make up a question to ask Mr. Dawson about formatting my senior research paper, but as for the others, how would I approach them? I don't know the janitor, I don't have Ms. Pasella for a class, and I don't play football."

"Express interest in joining the team," Lorilee said. "They're down a running back, so they might be happy to have a look at you."

"Yay." I rolled my eyes. "All my dreams are coming true."

"Surely you can speak to the janitor on some pretext. I'll see what I can do about meeting the English teacher, and I'll visit this store owner, Stu, and get a sense of the sort of person he is." She sniffed. "We certainly won't solve the crimes this way, but if we're lucky, we might pick up information that will convince Detective Law to turn away from Chris for a while and look in new directions."

To prepare for what she called our interviews (and what I thought of as fishing expeditions), we went online and looked up our targets. Lorilee took a free trial on a site that did background checks, and we learned that Stan Dailey, the assistant football coach, had a long history of late payments and defaulted loans. "There," she said triumphantly. "He obviously needs money."

"So you want me to ask him if he's paying his bills these days by encouraging B&Es?"

"Don't be facetious," Lorilee said irritably. "Bring up Ricky Fulmer and let him talk. You might be surprised at what you learn."

Erik Dawson, the computer teacher, was almost absent from the internet. We found only the most basic information: voter registration, property address, and listing as a member of the Linville High faculty. He didn't even have a photo on the school's website, as most teachers did.

"He's well aware of the dangers of the internet," I murmured. Did a man who protected his identity so closely do so because he was aware of how easy it was to disable other people's security systems? Perhaps because he had a hand in doing it himself?

Ms. Pasella, one of two English teachers, had an online presence that was pretty open. She'd been teaching at Linville for three years. She liked posting photos of herself on social media, usually with girlfriends at various restaurants and retreats, with a glass of wine in hand. Scanning her Facebook page, Lorilee said, "I know how I can arrange to meet her. I'll do my ditzy old lady bit."

The janitor, Mr. B, was actually Dean Bateman. I found him on two social media sites, and on both, his profile pic was the logo of a local band, Nother Day. It looked like he moonlighted as their roadie, and from the photos that were posted, I thought he was probably paid in cannabis. "He doesn't look like a criminal mastermind," was Lorilee's comment.

"I guess we'll find out tomorrow." *Or not*, I added inside my head. While I didn't think Lorilee and I could hurt anything by launching our own mini-investigation, I didn't have much hope that we'd make headway toward solving the crime by talking to randomly-selected suspects.

As I headed for my room and bed, I saw signs of a storm brewing in the living room. Red had found the Professor's chair empty and decided to jump up and take a nap. Now, the old cat stood on the floor below Red, his tail twitching like a willow tree in a strong wind. A low growl of warning from deep in his throat should have scared the newbie away, but Red wasn't budging. He had the high ground, and he intended to keep it.

All our permanent residents, feline and human, knew the Professor and his favorite chair were to be left alone. Red had definitely overstepped a boundary. Should I intervene, or wait to see what happened?

Before I could act, the situation resolved itself. With a lunge that belied his age, the Professor jumped onto the chair, hissing, and cuffed Red's head a few times. Red pressed against the chair back, hair bristling and eyes wide. He raised his paws threateningly, but before he decided how to proceed, the Professor had swatted him twice more. The blows were fairly light, like a boxer testing his opponent's nerve. A fierce growl said he was ready to do worse.

Getting the message, Red jumped to the floor, his ears flat against his head. Still puffed and angry, Professor Higgins glared down at him for a few seconds. Then he curled himself into a ball and settled down to smooth his coat with short licks that hinted he wasn't done being mad yet.

"I could have warned you," I told Red. "Nobody messes with the Professor."

At school Monday morning, I went looking for the pot-smoking janitor with a story about leaving my favorite sweatshirt at school on Friday. A little glassy-eyed but willing to be helpful, Mr. B led me to a storeroom where lost-and-found goods: shirts, sweaters, phones, clothing, jewelry, shoes, towels, even a prom dress, were all laid out neatly on a long table against one wall. I pretended to look for the shirt then shook my head. "It's got a picture of this local band that I like on the front," I told him. "Nother Day. Have you heard of them?"

"Bro, I'm *with* them," the guy crowed. "I do set-up and take-down. Sometimes they have me sit in on drums, cuz their regular guy is late, like, all the time."

"That's amazing."

"Bet." I let him talk for a while about his gigs with Nother Day, learning, among a bunch of other things, that he couldn't have been with Ricky the night he died, since he was with the band in Orlando. I sensed that Mr. B was probably not the boss of the Home-Hack Gang. He could barely remember the day's work schedule, and he looked forward only as far as the death metal music he'd be part of when his janitorial work was done. Thanking him, I went to find Birdy before the start of first period.

Chapter Twenty-Five

Lorilee

I held the door firmly as I entered Stu's StopNBuy a few minutes after one o'clock on Monday. The wind had come up strong, and it seemed determined to rip it out of my hands. I'd come during school hours, so I'd be able to speak to Stu without a bunch of kids around. He came through a curtained doorway, wearing a flour-speckled shirt and an irritated expression. "Help you?"

"I'm hoping you'll have salt and vinegar potato chips. I've looked at a half-dozen places, and they're all out."

"Over here." He led the way to a shelf crowded with miscellaneous snacks and pointed. "That what you want?"

"Yes, it is. Thank you so much." Taking the chips, I followed him to the cash register, paused at a warming table that displayed three kinds of pizza behind a glass shield. "You make pineapple-pepperoni pizza."

"Yup." He didn't say aloud that it was obvious, but his tone did.

"I'd love a slice of that. And I'll eat it here, if you don't mind."

"Okay with me." Stu, I glanced at his shirt and saw the name, got a plate, shoveled a slice of pizza out of the warmer, and handed it over the counter. I glanced at the tables in the corner, but since I didn't want to lose his attention, I simply picked up the slice and took a bite. It was greasy and tough, but I said, "Umm. Good."

We moved to the register, where I paid for the pizza and the bag of chips. "I don't think I've ever been in here," I said. "How long have you had the place?"

"Two years. Almost three."

Since he was released from prison after spending two years for stealing checks from an elderly relative and buying himself all sorts of gifts with them. I'd done my homework, and my subscription to the background check site was paying off nicely.

Gesturing at some photos on the wall behind him, I said, "Is that you in the football uniform?"

"Yeah. Played for Linville back in the day. Could've played in college, but I wrecked a shoulder my senior year." He rubbed the damaged joint. "My throwing arm, of course."

"I think I remember you," I said, making my tone admiring. "Stu Miller, right?" I'd memorized enough statistics to be convincing. "You led the Linville Lions to state finals in 2000."

"We'd have won it, except I got hurt."

"Tragic," I said sympathetically. "Not only for the team, but for your future in the sport. Didn't you have like 4,000 yards passing?"

"Junior year."

I shook my head. "My husband and I came to see you play a few times. He said you were a natural. It's not fair, what life does to a person sometimes."

"You got that right." Glancing around the crowded store as if reminded how low he'd fallen, he started telling me about his on-the-field accomplishments. I let him talk, adding an "Ooh" or an "Aah" when needed, while I tried to decide if he might have taught a couple of high school kids how to become burglars. He was certainly egotistical enough to be a criminal. As he spun tales of his football career, one might have concluded that back in the day, the Lions had had only one member.

Stu had the perfect setup for recruiting teens. They came into his place of business regularly, so he learned their names and their backgrounds. Watching and listening to them talk, he'd figure out who might be susceptible to dreams of wealth, or to images of daring deeds done at night.

When I had extended my visit for as long as I could, I told Stu how thrilled I was to have met him and turned to go. As I opened the door, I met Birdy coming in. She looked surprised to see me, but she stood back, holding the door against the wind so I could exit before she went in.

As I walked away, I checked my watch to be sure I was right. Two fifteen. What was Birdy doing at Stu's during school hours? It made no sense for her to skip a class and go to the local hangout all by herself. I concluded she'd probably been sent by a teacher to pick up pizza for some after-school activity.

I drove to the school, parked in the public lot out front, and waited until the dismissal bell rang. Students streamed from the building, fanning out in all directions, happy to be released from captivity. When the tide slowed, I got out of the car and made my way in, stopping, as directed by a sign in bold letters, to let the office know a stranger was in the building.

The secretary asked a student to escort me to Ms. Pasella's classroom. The teacher was getting ready to leave for the day. Her purse sat atop her desk, a stuffed-full tote bag beside it. "I'm sorry to stop in so late," I told her. "I'm Jesse Pall's guardian, and I wanted to make sure he's settling in well. He had bad experiences at his former school, so I'm hoping he does better here."

"Jesse," Ms. Pasella, a pretty woman of about thirty, glanced across the empty desks as if trying to imagine him. "I don't think he's one of mine."

I knew that. I was playing the confused old woman as an excuse to chat with her.

A girl of about fifteen sat at a table behind the teacher's desk. She looked faintly familiar, but I didn't recognize her until I heard her voice. "He's the kid with purple hair and an eyebrow stud, right?"

"That's him." She'd been at Ricky Fulmer's visitation. She was his cousin.

Striking a few keys, she said, "Jess has Mr. Daniels for English comp, second period."

"I'm sorry." I feigned confusion. "I heard him talking about English with Birdy, and I must have mixed up the teachers' names."

"Yes," Pasella said. "Birdy is in my fifth period class. I don't know Jesse, though now that Dylan mentioned the purple hair, I have seen him around."

After a few more keystrokes, Dylan said, "He got detention for fighting." Her tone was disapproving, and I pegged her as the Teacher's Pet type.

"That was cleared up. Jess and Chris Talbot were released from punishment when the real story came out."

"That's good," Pasella said. "Are those two friends?"

I frowned. "I wouldn't say so, but we live next door to the Talbots."

"Good." She pressed her lips together. "I mean, Chris is okay, but Jesse might want to look elsewhere for friends."

"Why do you say that?"

The teacher hesitated for a moment then said, "Dylan, I think we're done for the day. I'll see you tomorrow."

"Okay." Shutting down the computer, the girl left, the uneven sound of her footsteps reminding me that she had some kind of ankle injury.

"What's wrong with her foot?" I asked.

The teacher made a *tsk* sound. "The little goofball was at the dog park last weekend when a St. Bernard broke away from its owner and went after a puppy. Dylan jumped in and managed to hold the big dog back until the owners separated them, but his leash got tangled around her ankle and twisted it." She smiled. "I strongly suggested she stay out of dogfights in the future."

"Good advice." I returned to the comment she'd made earlier. "But about Chris Talbot. I heard the news reports, but when he wasn't charged with a crime, I assumed it was some kind of mistake. Do you believe he's dishonest?"

The teacher looked away. "I shouldn't say anything."

"I'm only concerned for Jess. If Chris can't be trusted, I'll do my best to steer the two of them apart." She didn't seem convinced, so I added, "I never had children, and I don't know the local kids. I need all the help I can get to see Jesse through his senior year and into college. I won't share what you tell me with anyone."

She sighed. "Dylan, the girl who just left, has been my assistant since last fall. As soon as I realized how smart she is, I told my husband about her. He runs a lawn care business that caters to upscale clients, and he was looking for an easy but reliable record-keeping system. Dylan was able to set one up for him."

I was wondering how that related to Chris, but she finally got there. "After … what happened to Ricky, Dylan came to me, very upset. She said last spring, Ricky and Chris asked her to let them have a look at my husband's customer list."

"Why?" Before the word was out of my mouth, I knew the answer. Mr. Pasella had a ready-made list of wealthy homeowners. He probably kept track of which houses were empty in the off-season. He might even know what kind of security systems they had, so his people didn't trip alarms as they worked. "What did Dylan do?"

"She said no, of course. She told Ricky she'd report him if he tried to hack the system, and she thought he had accepted that. But now she wonders whether she should tell the police about it."

"Of course she should."

Pasella shook her head. "It's not that simple. Ricky was the one who approached her about helping. Dylan can't remember if Ricky actually said Chris' name or if she assumed it was Chris when Ricky said 'we.' She

133

doesn't want to get Chris in more trouble when she isn't a hundred percent certain."

"I see."

"Besides that, Ricky and Dylan are cousins. She doesn't want her whole family mad at her, which they would be if she told."

I nodded. My visit to the funeral home had revealed a family united in belief in Ricky's innocence. "What did you do about it?"

"Dylan put a bunch of safeguards on my husband's site. We're certain that whatever those boys were doing, they didn't get their list of victims from us."

I sensed some wishful thinking there. It would be bad for business if the police learned the thieves' information had come from the lawn care company, so Pasella hoped more than knew that what she'd said was true. I doubted she would have pressed Dylan to take her story to the police.

The teacher's manner changed, and I guessed she was having second thoughts about what she'd told me. "I certainly don't mean to impugn Chris' reputation. I would simply recommend that since Jess is new here, he should be careful about who he hangs with."

"I'll pass that along." When her eyes widened, I added, "Without saying where I heard it."

Pasella seemed relieved. "Thanks. Sometimes a word of warning is warranted, I think."

"I appreciate your time, Ms. Pasella."

As I left the classroom, I lost track of where I was and ended up in a corridor that didn't seem right. As I stood at a crossing, trying to figure out which way led to where I'd left my car, a man stopped. "Can I help you?"

"I came in the main entrance, and a student took me to my destination. Now I'm confused about how to get out."

"I can show you." He chuckled. "I've often said they should color-code these hallways. They all look the same."

As we walked, he said, "I'm Don Gage, the guidance counselor here at Linville."

The man who'd given Jess detention without even asking for his side of the story. "Lorilee Riley. I'm Jesse Pall's guardian."

"Ah, the new boy. It was too bad he got into trouble last week, but luckily, we managed to sort things out."

No thanks to you, Mr. Detention-for-All. "Yes, it's good when adults step in to ensure fairness."

"Part of the job," he said with no apparent recognition of his failure to do exactly that. He opened a glass door for me, and we turned down a new hallway.

Since he seemed willing to talk, I encouraged him to comment on any or all of the boys he'd hosted in detention. "I spent my working years with Child and Family Services, so I saw quite a range of unacceptable behaviors."

Gage nodded vigorously. "They don't all come from great backgrounds. Rooster Kalamaris, the boy responsible for your ward's trouble, can be quite a trial." Probably fearful he'd sounded negative, he added, "I try to keep his unusual homelife in mind when I deal with him."

"Unusual?" I lifted my voice in that tone that says, *I'm interested.*

It worked. "Two years ago, the wife, who was the girl's mother and Rooster's stepmother, walked out on them. Since Mr. Kalamaris works in road construction, he's all over the state. The kids are left on their own a good deal of the time."

We'd come to the main doors, but I wasn't ready to leave yet. "You say the mother left the home?"

"Didn't tell a soul what she planned to do. Not even her own daughter." Gage opened the door for me. "You have a good rest of your day."

"Thanks. It was nice chatting with you."

My drive home was fraught with mental anguish. Birdy had been dishonest with Jess a second time. Failing to mention that Rooster was her stepbrother wasn't all that shocking, since I gathered he wasn't much of a prize. But this time, she'd definitely lied, telling both Jess and me that her mother was dead.

My problem was whether to tell Jess what I'd learned or let him find out on his own. Did Birdy's falsehoods indicate a dishonest personality, or was it something else? That led to questions I didn't want to face: Was I crazy for taking in a teenager in the first place at my age? And was I crazy for wishing I could spare Jess the pain of Birdy's betrayal? I was afraid my favorite teenager was about to get his heart broken.

At home, I set all that aside, took a deep breath, and called the sheriff's department. "This is Lorilee Riley , and I'm hoping to speak to Detective Law."

The man informed me that Law was currently unavailable, so I gave my number and asked that he call me. It took almost an hour, but he did.

"Ms. Riley . Jim Law. What's up?"

"Hello, Detective. I've come across some information on the death of Ricky Fulmer, and I wanted to pass it on."

"How did you get this information?"

"I can't say. I'm passing it on for you to do with as you wish."

"Okay. What have you got?"

"It's possible there was an adult behind the robberies Ricky Fulmer was involved in, someone who planned the crimes and then sent teenage boys in to do the actual work."

"Fulmer and Talbot."

"I'm not sure Talbot was there, but if you find the person who planned the crimes, that will lead to the correct arrests."

"So who is this mastermind?"

"A name I heard was Stuart Miller. He runs a convenience store near the high school."

"And how do you know he's the one?"

"I don't, Detective. I'm asking you to look into his activities and find out if he is."

"You can't tell me where this information comes from?"

"Um, no."

He sighed. "I'll take a look at Miller's record. But I'd need a lot more than this to take action." A voice spoke in the background, and Law said, "I have to go, Ms. Riley. We intercepted a big drug shipment yesterday, and there's a ton of work involved in pinning down all the evidence."

"Thank you, Detective." I hung up with the feeling that my attempt to interest Law in a shadowy figure behind the Home-Hack Gang's activities had been unsuccessful. He had another crime to work on, and it sounded bigger than a few home invasions. He also had a convenient theory that Chris was the remaining guilty party. And while he hadn't yet nailed him for it, I sensed that was where his focus was.

Chapter Twenty-Six

Jess

The walk home from the shelter Monday night was gorgeous. The winds had calmed after sweeping away every wisp of clouds, so the sky was bright with stars. The temperature was perfect for walking, around sixty degrees. I passed the Talbots' place, where every window was lit. What were they doing? I wondered. Probably not having family game night or singing around the piano. It was a house full of people who didn't relate to each other in any meaningful way.

Lorilee had texted to say that Red's family came for him. They were living in half their house, but once they found out he was alive, they couldn't wait to get him back. She'd ended her text with, *Prof is much relieved.*

When I got home, she was repairing tears in the living room drapes with duct tape. "No sense replacing them until Orange is gone," she said cheerfully. "I wonder if she's always been a curtain climber or if it's a reaction to trauma."

The drapes on the big living room window looked like someone had fired a shotgun through them—maybe three or four blasts. We always took Orange off them when we saw her there, untangling her claws from the fabric and giving her a few words of reprimand. It hadn't worked, and in the end, Lorilee said it was time for new drapes anyway. I got out the stepladder and climbed up to mend the tears higher up, where Lorilee couldn't easily reach.

As we worked, I noticed that Lorilee talked nonstop. She recounted the day's events in detail. She'd been making lunch when Mayson and Orange got into a snarling match. When she'd gone to stop that, Red had climbed up on the counter and stolen her sandwich. She theorized that the cat had been fed from the table in his former home. She shook her head at that practice, saying it was best that he was now back home in Fort Myers. Then she turned to Violet's oddness. She stayed under the bed ninety-nine percent of the time, and Lorilee said we were lucky she was brave enough to come out to use the litter box. It would be a pain to clean up cat dirt under the bed.

None of it was unusual, except tonight it seemed drawn out. I also noticed that Lorilee avoided looking me in the eye, and her hands moved all the time, touching her chin, her elbows, her shoulders. Like she couldn't make them be still.

Finally, I said, "Why don't you tell me what's on your mind?"

She started with Ms. Pasella and her warning that Chris couldn't be trusted. She told me about Mr. Gage, who'd helped her find the right exit. She said she'd met Stu, the convenience store owner, and found him dull, possibly too much so to be a criminal mastermind. Then, unwillingly, Lorilee recounted her conversation with Mr. Gage, who had revealed Birdy's lie. Her mother was not dead. She had abandoned her husband, her step-son, and her own daughter.

Though I immediately felt bad for Birdy, I also felt angry. Why couldn't she simply tell the truth?

Could I continue to be friends with a girl who'd lied to my face, twice? While not mentioning that Rooster was her step-brother hadn't been an out-and-out lie, it was kind of important to me to know that she lived with the guy most likely to beat me up if he got the chance. What if I'd dropped by to see her and Rooster had answered the door?

This lie was worse. Birdy had clearly told us her mother was dead.

We worked silently for a while. The only sound in the room was the rip of duct tape. "What do you think I should do?" I asked.

"I don't know," Lorilee replied. "It sounds like she's had it rough, so maybe you just go on being her friend."

"How can I be her friend if she lies all the time?"

"Don't exaggerate, Jess. Twice is not 'all the time.'"

"But what if she's being friendly to me for a reason?"

"Like what?"

"Like finding out what Chris is telling people about the robberies and the accident." A theory formed in my head. "Rooster and Ricky were friends. He could have been the one in the car with Ricky."

Lorilee handed me another strip of tape. "I'm sure the police looked into where all of Ricky's friends were that night."

"But what if Birdy lied for Rooster? She said once she knows things that could get him in trouble. What if they're all in on it, Chris and Ricky and Rooster and Birdy? They already tried once to make me a suspect."

"It was Mitzi who sicced the cops on you, not Chris." She considered what I'd said for a moment. "This Rooster sounds more likely to go into crime than Chris. He apparently has very little support at home, either financially or emotionally. You say he's aggressive with everyone, so he might feel like the world is against him and he's owed something."

"If Rooster did pull those robberies with Ricky, that explains why he's bad-mouthing Chris every chance he gets." I went on, though it hurt me to say it. "If Birdy's in on it with them, she deliberately got me on her side by helping with Gage. She might be trying to find out from me how much Ricky told Chris about the scheme."

Lorilee agreed it was a possibility. "You live next door to Chris, and you came to his defense at school. From that they might conclude that you two are friends." Lorilee tapped her roll of duct tape with a finger. "I wonder if you could reverse things on them and use your friendship with Birdy to find out who Fagin is."

It felt like a betrayal, pumping Birdy for information, but then again, if she wasn't playing me, it wouldn't be like that. Folding the stepladder, I said, "I can try. But I'll be careful what I tell Birdy until we know for sure she isn't one of them."

Sadness in Lorilee's eyes told me she felt sorry for me, but all she said was, "I suppose that's wise."

I had a restless night, arguing with myself about what Birdy was really like. Old fears about myself returned. How could I have believed a girl would find me interesting? Dad had certainly told me often enough that I needed to change if I wanted to be popular with "the ladies." Was he right? Did Birdy chuckle with her stepbrother about the skinny kid who talked about cats and never went to pep rallies?

At one point I thought about sending a breakup by text: *You lied, so don't ever talk to me again.* But that was the coward's way, and disgusting besides. Lorilee wanted me to use my friendship with Birdy to get information, but that didn't feel right either.

In the end, I decided that even if she couldn't be honest with me, I would be honest with her. I really liked Birdy, and that meant I had to give her a chance to explain herself.

Chapter Twenty-Seven

Lorilee

I took a plate of cinnamon rolls to the shelter on Tuesday, where things were starting to settle down. The animals were healing from wounds and recovering from the trauma they'd experienced. Each day, one or two went home or joined their families in some temporary housing situation. Some would relocate permanently, but at least they were back with the humans they loved.

There were sad cases, families who simply couldn't take their pets back or people who were injured and unable to care for them. Dr. Ahuja assured those callers that he'd do his best to rehome the homeless and care for the others until circumstances allowed them to reunite. The vet would never become wealthy with the way he ran his business, but he was certainly loved, by both animals and people.

Back at home, I tackled litter pan duty. Not to be indelicate, but the more cats one has, the bigger the smell, the more frequent the need for scooping, and the heavier the disposal bag. As I dumped a large trash bag of stinky nuggets outside the back door, I heard a knock at the front. I hurried to see who'd come calling, pausing briefly for a spritz of hand sanitizer on the way.

Alicia Kendall, head of the homeowners' association, stood on my porch, her hand raised to knock a second time. Tiny, gray-haired, and prim, I always thought she could have commanded a battleship using only her steel-gray eyes and a few terse words. She wore Florida business casual clothing, a crisp white top over coral Capris and woven sandals. Under her arm was a clipboard, no doubt brought along to remind me of the wording of the agreement reached between the association, the Talbots, and me.

"Good morning, Lorilee," she said crisply. "May we talk?"

"Of course, Alicia." I stepped onto the porch and closed the door before she could see inside. "Would you like to sit on the patio? It's nice out there this time of day."

"No, thank you. This shouldn't take long."

Her purpose might have been an appeal for funds for some worthy cause, but I doubted it. Alicia's single-minded pursuit of fairness meant she was routinely elected to run the association. Her credo: *There are rules. Rules are for everyone. Everyone must observe them.* When someone didn't, she wasn't shy about pointing it out. I had no doubt that the reason for Alicia's visit was the rule that had been drafted and agreed upon specifically for me.

"We've received a complaint," she said in her usual, dry tone. "While I don't mean to inconvenience you, we have to investigate such things, or what good is the association?"

"I understand. What's the problem?"

Instead of answering, she handed me a printout of the letter she'd received.

Homeowner People

Lorilee Rileys keeping more cats than shes sposed to. You had better go over there and do something about it.

Signed,

Mitzi Talbot

"I doubt Mitzi sent this," I told Alicia. "It sounds more like her son Greg."

"That's exactly what I think." Her eyes met mine. "Is it true?"

I could have argued that the only way Greg could know I had extra cats was by trespassing. I could have said it was wrong to let a ten-year-old harass me. I could have fought it, but I simply didn't have the energy.

"Look," I said. "The local vet is swamped with dogs and cats he rescued after Hurricane Ian. I offered to take in a half-dozen healthy cats until he can either locate their owners or find them new homes. It isn't permanent. In fact, four of them are already gone. I wasn't trying to violate the rules of the HA. I simply did my part to help after that horrible storm down south."

Alicia stood very still for a few seconds, her eyes unfocused and her clipboard clutched to her chest. I had admitted to breaching the rule. I wondered what my punishment would be. A fine? No problem, I'd pay whatever they decided. What else could they do to me? Kick me out after all these years? If they tried, I'd have my niece the attorney sue their collective pants off.

"You say this vet has dogs as well as cats?"

"Um, yes."

It was the first time I'd ever seen the old girl's teeth. With a smile that turned her militant manner a hundred-eighty degrees, she said, "I need to get down there. My daughter's dog got scared and ran away during the storm. Their house sustained damage, so my grandkids are staying with me while Sally and her husband make repairs." Her steel-gray eyes warmed to polished nickel. "The kids are devastated to have lost Burt, but he could be right here in Linville."

"Even if he isn't," I said, "Dr. Ahuja can help you find him. Local vets and animal organizations are sharing information, and they even have a facial recognition site set up online to help people find lost pets."

"Wonderful!" Remembering the purpose of her visit, Alicia tapped the letter she'd shown me, now clipped to the board, with an unvarnished fingernail. "I'll tell the committee you need a temporary suspension of the eight-cat rule. I'm sure they'll understand that the situation calls for it." The board would do whatever Alicia told them to, but that was fine with me. "Then," she went on, "I'm going to see that the little monster next door understands that he can't get away with things like this."

It was my chance to get back at Nasty Greg for all the spying and snooping and tattling and harassment, but thinking of Mitzi's tears, Chris' air of depression, and the possibility of more trouble to come, I knew it wasn't the right time for revenge. "They have a lot going on right now," I told Alicia. "If you don't mind, let's let this one slide."

Chapter Twenty-Eight

Jess

As I walked to school on Tuesday, my phone beeped with a text from Birdy. *Busy 2day. My turn 2 run schl store. Errand after. See U tmrow.*

I wrote back, *Wll wlk w/U after. Hve smethng to ask U.*

A few seconds later: *U'll B lte 4 wrk.*

Plenty of tme, I wrote back. That wasn't exactly true, but I figured once we had it out about her lies, I'd run all the way to the shelter.

The day went by both too quickly and too slowly. I dreaded the coming confrontation, but I wanted to get it over with too. My mind kept making excuses for Birdy's latest lie. Maybe her mom had left home and then died. Maybe Mr. Gage had her mixed up with some other student. Maybe I'd misunderstood what she said.

When school dismissed that afternoon, Birdy came out of the building, shielding her eyes from the bright sun as she searched the crowd. Seeing me, she smiled, and I made myself smile back. She pointed in a direction, and we fell into step together.

Once we'd moved away from the crowd, I said, "Tell me about your mom, Birdy."

Her step faltered, but she caught herself quickly. She didn't ask what I meant. She knew. "I didn't mean to—" Her lips quivered, and she pressed them tightly together.

"You can tell me," I said.

After a few seconds, she spoke in a low voice. "When I was thirteen, my mom, who I loved more than anyone in the whole world, waited until there was a Saturday afternoon when we were all gone from home." She smiled grimly. "Dave had to work. Rooster was playing in a softball tournament. I went to a friend's birthday party." Her voice wavered as she said, "I remember it was a really nice party, and I had so much fun." Birdy sniffed lightly. "Anyway, while we were gone, Mom packed one suitcase and took off. She didn't leave a note. She never once hinted to me that she was thinking about leaving. Obviously, she didn't feel a need to take me along." Birdy looked at me, her eyes full of unshed tears. "That's why I tell people she's dead. Because she *is* dead to me."

It felt like I should say something, but I had no idea what it should be. I thought I had suffered a lot, but my dad's bullying was nothing compared to a mother who'd sneak away and leave her only child behind. "I'm sorry."

Birdy blinked her tears away. "I'm over it. You have to move on, right?"

"Right." It didn't feel like enough to say, but it was all I had.

The errand she'd mentioned was at the cable office. When we got there, Birdy said I should wait outside. Checking the time on my phone, I watched as she spoke to the woman behind the desk. Birdy was friendly, but the woman appeared to be short with her. Birdy's chin rose, and I saw a flush of red creep up her cheeks as she explained something. The woman gave her a dirty look, but in the end, she took an envelope Birdy offered, holding it as if she'd like to drop it in the nearest wastebasket.

When she came back outside, Birdy's lips were tight. "Done."

"Is everything okay?"

She rubbed her sleeve across her nose. "You know how it is. Money only stretches so far."

Actually, I didn't know how that was. My parents were financially comfortable, and Lorilee was loaded, though not many people knew it. The accident that had killed her husband and messed her up resulted in a settlement that meant she'd never have to worry about money.

"We haven't got a lot," Birdy said without looking at me. "Our house isn't nice like yours. In fact, it's pretty bad."

"Hey, as long as people are honest, they're okay to me."

"Honesty doesn't pay the bills," she said in a hard tone. "Sometimes people get tired of never having enough."

Trying for a light tone, I asked, "Do you long for diamond earrings and golden bracelets?"

That got me a swat on the arm, but she did smile. "I don't like jewelry. It gets in the way when you're trying to get things done. But I think Rooster's always-on-the-muscle attitude is partly embarrassment about the way we live. He's got no car, we've got government-issue phones, and we shop at Goodwill. Typical Florida rednecks." After a pause, she added, "I know Rooster's a jerk, but I watch out for him when I can. I don't want him to mess up his life before he even gets out of high school."

Sensing Birdy was done with that topic, I told her about Howie the Parrot, who'd been picked up the day before by his owner, an older guy whose house had been flattened by the hurricane. "They're going up north to live with the man's daughter and her family," I said. "I'm guessing there will be trouble in that house if Howie doesn't learn to shut up."

Birdy didn't say much for a while, but as I went on, telling funny stories about the animals, her mood lifted a little. I thought about how hard her life must be, bargaining with her stepfather's creditors and being treated with disrespect and snide remarks. I thought about how hard it must be to live all day, every day with Rooster, who probably wasn't any nicer at home than he was at school. I tried to understand how a person in that position might gloss over details of her life, possibly so people wouldn't pity her quite so much.

The disturbing part of that was the question of how much Birdy would do to escape the endless need for money to pay the bills. Would she agree to be part of a burglary ring? Or keep quiet about her stepbrother's participation? How many lies was she willing to tell to change the conditions in her life?

By the time Birdy and I separated, I had to run to get to work on time. When I got to the shelter, puffing and sweaty, an older couple stood at the front desk, talking to the receptionist. "This is the guy you need to talk to," she told them. To me, she said, "These folks are here to pick up their cat."

"We'll only be in Florida until tomorrow morning," the woman explained. "Our trailer park was destroyed, so we're going back to Michigan. We've hung around this long, hoping we wouldn't have to leave without Felix." She held out her phone to show me a photo. It was Indigo.

"I know that guy," I told them. "He's staying at my house."

"Oohhhh!" The woman stepped toward me, arms outstretched. "We can't thank you enough for keeping him for us," she said, hugging me until I wondered if I'd ever get to breathe again.

When she stepped back, the man shook my hand. "Never thought I'd miss that little bundle of energy," he said, "but it's sure good to know we're going to have him back with us. Thank you."

"No problem," I said. "I—we like cats."

"We're going to go to the nearest pet store right now and buy a carrier and whatever else he'll need for the trip," the woman said. "Could we pick him up in the morning, before we start north?"

"Sure." Taking her phone, I put our address into the GPS. "We're up early."

"It's been a terrible time," she said, "but it's great that we found our cat. We'll leave a financial donation for the shelter, but if there's anything else we can do to help, we'd love to hear it."

"Where will you be living up north?" I asked.

"We have a house outside Lansing."

"Got lots of room?"

She chuckled. "More than we need for two old people and a cat."

"Then there is something you could do. Felix has made a friend at our house, and his family isn't able to keep him. I think Felix would be really happy if Yellow went home with him."

The woman looked at her husband, who shrugged to indicate it was okay with him. She patted my arm. "Then I guess we'll buy two cat carriers and twice the kibble for the trip home."

Chapter Twenty-Nine

Jess

Wednesday morning, Birdy wasn't waiting where we usually met outside the school. I didn't think much of it, since there was a drizzly rain falling. Inside the building, I went to the hall where her locker was. She wasn't there, but I caught a glimpse of her up ahead. When I called, she didn't turn but hurried on. I almost caught up, but she disappeared into the girls' bathroom. I stopped at the doorway, wondering whether I should wait for her to come out. When two girls exited and gave me a look that said they thought I was a perv trying to get a look inside, I turned away. The bell rang, signaling it was time to get to class, so I left, wondering whether Birdy hadn't known I was there or was avoiding me.

At lunchtime the rain had stopped, but Birdy was nowhere to be seen. I ate my lunch alone, wondering what was going on. Was she mad because I'd found out about her weird family? I'd tried to let her know I understood. It wasn't like I had normal parents either.

When Birdy wasn't sitting outside the building at the end of the day, I knew something was wrong. After a few minutes, when it was clear she was avoiding me, I started for the shelter, feeling like what I'd heard guys say for years was true. It's hard to figure out what a woman wants.

Work is a good antidote for worry. I was busy enough that afternoon that Birdy's actions faded into the back of my mind, something I could puzzle out later. At nine, I finished work, locked the shelter, and started for home. My feet ached from all the running I'd done, including assisting with two surgeries then doing my cleaning and set-up for the next day's business. A couple more extra dogs had been claimed, so I had scrubbed the cages clean and disinfected them thoroughly.

"Jess?" The voice from the shadows made me jump, and I turned, squinting into the dark. "It's me. Chris."

"Hey, man. What's up?"

"Have you heard from Birdy since school?" Chris stepped closer. "I ... I'm worried about her."

"Worried? Why?"

"I think Stu asked her to take Ricky's place."

"What? Why do you think that?"

"After school today, I went by the store and saw her going in. She looked ... I don't know ... serious, you know? It seemed weird, so I hung around for a while and watched. The other kids sat at the tables and gabbed, but Birdy and Stu went off by themselves, like Stu and Ricky used to do. They talked for a long time." He paused. "Did Lorilee tell you about Stu?"

"I know she suspects he's behind the robberies."

"Like I told her, Stu and Ricky got real close last spring. They'd talk in corners and do dumb stuff like secret handshakes." He wiped his nose with the back of his hand. "Today, Stu did most of the talking. At first, Birdy seemed to be saying no, but after a while, she nodded, like 'Yeah, I'll do it.' When she left, Stu walked her to the door, and I heard him say, 'Be here at closing time.'"

I looked up at the security light for a few seconds, mulling it over. "I think we need to be there at closing time too."

"That's ten on weekdays." Chris checked his phone. "We've got about twenty minutes."

"Let me tell Lorilee what's going on."

"I'll go with you."

Lorilee seemed surprised to see Chris, but she listened as he repeated what he'd told me. "Jess and I think we need to be there," he finished.

"Shouldn't we call the police?"

"What would we tell them? A girl we know is talking to a guy and we don't like it?"

"You're right. We have no proof there's anything wrong with that. I suppose the two of you might find out something more damning if you're careful." Though Lorilee had mentioned talking to Chris before, I was surprised at how well they seemed to know and trust each other. "I'm not thrilled with the idea, but I can't think of another way to prove that Stu is involved in the crimes."

"And we have to make sure Birdy's okay," Chris said.

Lorilee seemed torn, but after a moment she told us, somewhat reluctantly, about seeing Birdy at the convenience store the day she'd gone there to meet Stu. Though she didn't say it aloud, I guessed Lorilee thought Birdy might have been there when no other students were around so that she and Stu could plan a crime in private.

Was Birdy part of the Home-Hack Gang? My hope was that if she was considering it, she hadn't actually joined yet. If we got Detective Law on the case before she participated in a robbery, I thought she'd be okay.

Why would she do it? I asked myself, but there were several good answers. Like her stepbrother, Birdy didn't have great clothes, fancy gadgets, or spending cash. Even if she didn't want that stuff, Birdy was desperate to go to college, and that took money.

Stop it! I gave myself a mental shake. Birdy *isn't a thief. She's got some kind of plan. She didn't want me involved, and that's why she avoided me earlier.*

"We have to go and see what we can find out," I told Lorilee. "We'll call the cops if anything looks shady."

"Do that," Lorilee said. Chris and I left her on the couch, stroking Callie and looking unhappy. We started for Stu's.

"So you knew local kids were taking part in those robberies?"

Chris nodded. "Ricky hinted he could get me into something that made money, but I said no."

"Who's in on it?"

"Honestly, aside from Ricky I have no idea. When Stu shoved me up against that wall and said to keep my mouth shut, I realized he was part of it. Who the others are, how many there are, no clue."

We walked on for a while, and Chris said, "I wouldn't think Birdy would join them."

I was struggling with that myself, and I'd come up with a theory. "What if she's trying to prove you're innocent by finding the real thieves?"

"Dude, you think she'd do that?"

"I can't picture Birdy robbing anyone, so I'd say she's got a secret motive. I think she's trying to help you out."

While it was better than Birdy being a thief, that explanation bothered me. First, she was playing with fire. I knew first-hand how dangerous it could be to corner a desperate criminal. Second, I couldn't see how she'd prove that Chris was innocent by joining the gang. And third, sadly, I was back to being jealous. Birdy was sticking her neck out for Chris. What did he have that I didn't? I mean, besides big shoulders, washboard abs, and a killer smile?

"Why do you think he asked her to come back tonight?" I asked as we approached Stu's place.

"According to what Ricky told me, someone other than Stu decides if a person is the type they're looking for."

"At least we'll be there in case there's trouble."

"Right. If she needs help, you can call the cops."

"Why me?"

Chris whacked me on the arm. "Dude, do you think they'd believe me? I'm their Number One Suspect."

Chapter Thirty

Lorilee

After Jess and Chris left, I couldn't sit still. My mind buzzed with possibilities, none of them happy. While the boys had promised they'd only watch to see that Birdy was safe, I knew how quickly plans go awry when you're making them up as you go.

I kept thinking I should call the police, but Jess was right. A girl meeting a man at his place of business was no big deal. He might be hiring her as a clerk. They might be discussing politics. There could be a surprise party in the works for someone they knew. A host of innocuous excuses, if that's what was needed.

Though the boys had promised to report what they saw, my phone remained blank and silent. Typing with my index finger, which always made Jess smile, I sent a message. *Do not fail to keep me informed.* A second later I got that most irritating of responses: *K*

I took Fat Albert on my lap. While he isn't my usual cuddle companion, it felt like I needed his bulk to hold me in place. Out there were two boys I cared about, one desperate to protect the girl he loved, and the other desperately hoping to find something that would keep him out of jail.

And even with a small army of cats for support, I couldn't figure out how to help either of them.

Chapter Thirty-One

Jess

Birdy was at the side door of Stu's store when Chris and I arrived. We stopped in the shadows as she knocked softly, and Stu came, smiling, to usher her inside. He'd turned off most of the lights, so we strained to see them, Birdy's pale t-shirt and Stu's blond hair the most visible elements. They spoke for some time, and Chris said, "We should have got closer, so we could hear."

"I doubt we'd hear anything with the place all closed up."

"Let's at least get on the same side of the street." Without waiting for me to respond, he scurried across, staying out of the light. I followed, but we gained nothing. In fact, we could no longer see inside at all, since the window we crouched under was high and small.

"Bad idea." Chris seemed disgusted with himself, but then the front door opened, and Birdy and Stu stepped outside. Flattening ourselves against the wall, we slid along the side of the building to a spot that was unlit.

I heard the clink of keys as Stu locked up. "My truck's parked in back," he said. Turning my head, I saw a Ford short-box with lots of chrome parked in the far corner of the lot, next to the trash bins. The chirp of the remote sounded, the headlights flashed, and the doors unlocked with a clunk.

"What do we do?" Chris said in my ear.

"I don't know. We've got no way to follow them."

"Then we have to go along." Bending quickly, Chris picked up a handful of the decorative pumice stones laid along the building to discourage weeds. "As soon as they turn away, run to the back of Stu's truck and hunch down."

Without waiting for discussion, Chris tossed a few stones in a high arc. They landed on the street behind Stu and Birdy, making a clatter. When they turned to look behind them, Chris took off, and I followed. By the time Stu and Birdy came toward us again, we were both squatting at the back of the pickup. Chris had a second handful of stones, and he threw them in the direction of the store roof. They hit with a rat-tat-tat, making little rumbles as they bumped and bounced to the ground. Stu and Birdy stopped again, turning toward the noise. While they were distracted, Chris and I crawled over the tailgate and onto the truck bed. My hands felt the smooth surface of the bedliner, and my nose, pressed into it, caught the rubbery scent. The liner was new, like the truck. I guessed that stolen goods had paid for Stu's new ride.

When it was quiet again, Stu and Birdy approached the truck. I held my breath, hoping neither would glance into the back and see us there. If Birdy saw us, what would she do? That depended on her purpose for contacting Stu, and while I told myself it was innocent, I didn't know that for sure. Not yet.

Acting the gentleman, Stu opened the passenger door for Birdy and waited while she settled herself inside. Chris blew a sigh of relief when her door closed, but I waited until Stu got in on my side before I let myself believe we were okay.

The engine started, and the pickup pulled smoothly onto the street. Turning over onto my back, I texted Lorilee: *Flwing Brdy n Stu*. She wouldn't like it if she knew *how* we were following, but what else could we do?

Stu navigated onto Main Street, through town, and onto a county road leading out of Linville. Each stop at a corner or a red light was terrifying, since if one of them looked behind them, we'd be clearly visible under the streetlights. Stu followed the county road for a few miles, then turned off onto a narrower, darker road. Finally, he turned again, this time onto an unpaved lane that ran between fences. One more turn, and he stopped the truck, got out, and went around to open Birdy's door. "This is it."

"There's nobody here." Birdy sounded nervous. "I thought you were taking me to meet—"

"The boss, right. This is better than the store, I guess."

It was torture to stay where we were, with our faces pressed to the bedliner, but we didn't dare raise our heads in case Stu looked back. After a few seconds, I heard a squeal, followed by a grind that started, stopped, ground again, and stopped with an abrupt squeak. I recognized the sound of a sliding door, the wooden kind used on barns and sheds. It had opened and then closed again as Birdy and Stu went inside some structure.

Chris and I rose slowly to a crouch, peering through the truck's windows at an old Quonset hut, a half-circle of corrugated metal about twenty feet high at its apex. The enclosed end, made of rough boards with a door and two windows cut into it, faced us. A slightly crooked mercury lamp hung over the door, casting a bluish light over fifty or more orange crates piled haphazardly to one side of the door. A storage barn for an orange grove, I concluded, but from the general air of dilapidation, no longer in use.

"Call the sheriff," Chris said in a low voice. "Tell them Birdy's in trouble."

Taking out my phone, I first texted Lorilee: *stopt @ old Quonset hut in boonies.* Then I called 911. When the dispatcher answered, I said, "I'm reporting an abduction. A man named Stuart Miller took my girlfr—my friend—to an abandoned building out in the country somewhere near Linville." At first the dispatcher took my call seriously, but when she began asking specific questions, I realized how little I knew. I had no idea where we were. I couldn't explain why I'd hitched a ride. And I had to admit Birdy came with Stu willingly.

After a pause that didn't bode well, the woman asked, "Your name?"

"Um, Jesse Pall. I'm a friend of B—Ms. Byrd."

"Mr. Pall, you say Ms. Byrd came to this spot voluntarily?"

"Yeah, kinda, but she's in trouble. The guy is responsible for the Home-Hack burglaries the police are investigating."

"How do you know that?"

"I—um—He threatened Chris Talbot, and—"

"Talbot. Isn't that the boy who was questioned about those crimes?"

"Well, yes, but—"

"Mr. Pall—"

The dispatcher had concluded I was a jealous boyfriend. Bringing Chris' name into it had made her even more suspicious. "Look, will you call Detective James Law please? Ask him to contact Lorilee Riley right away. She can explain everything, but it needs to happen now. Birdy's in danger."

"I'll speak to my supervisor. If you can stay on the line—"

Chris jabbed my shoulder with a knuckle and pointed toward the Quonset hut. "We gotta see what's going on in there."

I nodded. To the dispatcher, I said, "I'm sorry, but I can't. Please tell Detective Law that Jess needs him to talk to Lorilee as soon as possible." I ended the call.

"Are they coming?"

"It might take a while. Once they confirm with Lorilee, they'll have to locate us, and then they have to get here." A thought scratched repeatedly at the back of my mind. When the police arrived, would they rescue Birdy or arrest her? I wished I knew why she'd agreed to come out here with Stu.

Chris didn't seem worried about Birdy's motives. "Let's go. We need to get her out of there."

I followed him over the tailgate and toward the building. When we got close, he veered right and made his way along the curved metal side, using his phone as a flashlight. I did the same, stepping carefully so I didn't make a noise or trip and fall. We passed under some spindly-looking orange trees, and I ducked low, imagining aphids, stinkbugs, and other citrus pests sliding down my neck in the darkness.

At the back of the building were two windows. Shutting down our phone lights, we peered inside, where a battery-operated lantern hung on an upright post, casting a small circle of light. In its spill, Birdy sat on an upturned orange crate, looking nervous. Stu leaned against the post, apparently at ease. They were obviously waiting, and for a while, neither said anything.

I looked the place over, trying to plan a way we might get Birdy out of there. The only entrance was the sliding door at the front. I counted four windows, two each in front and back, but they had been covered with chicken wire to keep animals out. The interior space, perhaps fifty feet long, was mostly empty, with a few pieces of what looked like discarded equipment pushed off to the sides. I recognized a tiller with a broken tine and some vintage smudge pots, but nothing else looked familiar. Several coils of hose lay along the right-hand wall, possibly soakers. Modern groves had more efficient methods, like sprinklers and drip systems. This was a piece of old Florida, frozen in time.

When Stu spoke, Chris and I set our backs to the wall and each put an ear as close to the window as we could without risking being seen. I heard most of what was said, though Birdy's voice was lower than Stu's. She was definitely not comfortable in this place.

"Cold in here," Stu said. "You shoulda brought a jacket." I took a quick look and saw that Birdy sat with arms crossed, her elbows cupped in her hands. If she was shivering, I guessed the cold night was only half the cause. "So you think your brother isn't right for this job."

"Like I told you, Rooster can't follow orders and he can't keep his mouth shut. You go with him, he'll end up getting arrested, and you won't be far behind." She pointed at herself. "I know how to do both, and I want to be able to buy stuff, like Ricky did. A decent phone. Some nice jewelry."

The out-of-character tone, boastful claims, and greediness of her statement actually relieved my mind. I knew Birdy didn't want "nice jewelry." That meant she had no intention of joining the Home-Hack Gang. She'd stepped in to keep her numbskull stepbrother out of trouble, not because she was fond of him, but because she felt responsible for him. Once she learned who the players were in the string of robberies, I guessed she planned to go to the police.

"Did Rooster tell you I talked to him?"

"I heard him on the phone last night, and he mentioned doing Ricky's job. He said your name once, so I put two and two together."

"He likes the idea of all that money," Stu said agreeably. "But we aren't sure he's the right guy. Ricky was careful."

"Rooster isn't." Birdy's tone became more confident. "He loves taking chances, and you can bet that sooner or later, he'll do something dumb."

"That was kinda my impression."

"I can do what Ricky did. You'll be back on track in no time."

"Little girl, I have doubts about your honesty." He chuckled. "I should say doubts about your *dis*honesty. You're kinda known for never doing anything wrong." His tone changed. "I hope you aren't lying to me, or Birdy might get her wings clipped."

Birdy made an odd noise, and I tensed, ready to jump through the window if Stu had laid a hand on her. Stealing a glance, Chris whispered, "He's got a knife, Jess. We gotta do something."

A hand touched my arm, and I almost yelped in surprise. Turning, I saw— sensed, really—a presence between Chris and me. A voice whispered, "What are you guys doing?"

Chris recognized her. "Dylan! You about gave me a heart attack."

"How'd you get here?" I asked.

"I was driving through town when I saw you two crawl into Stu's truck. I decided to follow, in case somebody needed help."

"We definitely need help."

"Good, because I brought this." She pulled something from her waistband.

I wasn't sure I was seeing what I thought I was seeing. "Is that a gun?"

"It is."

"It beats Stu's knife," Chris commented hopefully.

Then I felt the cold metal of the barrel touch my temple. "Sorry," Dylan said, "but I wasn't thinking of helping *you*. I came to bail out my old buddy Stu."

"Stu's a criminal," Chris whispered. "We're going to—"

"Go inside and tell him all about it," Dylan finished for him.

A minute later, we were inside the Quonset hut, perched on orange crates Stu set on either side of the one Birdy sat on. Dylan searched us, took our phones, and powered them down, using her jacket sleeve to keep from leaving prints. She set them on a brace board, where they teased us with possibilities. Too late now to call the police with more specific information on the threat we faced.

Chris and I were silent, ashamed to have been taken so easily. Birdy wasn't silent at all. "I thought you were cool, Dylan. I thought—" She shook her head. "Never mind. You're a punk."

"I'm getting to be pretty well off for a punk, while you're breaking your neck to get some pathetic scholarship."

Birdy shook her head. "You could have done something good with your skills. Why break the law working for a guy like Stu?"

Dylan laughed, a silvery sound I remembered liking the first time I heard it. "I don't work for Stu, Birdy. Stu works for me."

"You're the boss he was talking about?"

Stu seemed to enjoy our stunned expressions, and he explained. "Ricky used to help me stock shelves sometimes to earn a few bucks. He liked to hear about some of the not-legal things I've done. We talked about how easy it would be to rob those rich-bitch homes in Tampa if it weren't for all the alarms and stuff. One day Ricky says, "My cousin knows all about computers. She says she could shut all that stuff down, and then we could just go in and take what we want.""

Birdy turned to Dylan. "So you became the brains."

"Ricky had the nerve. And from his time in prison, Stu here had contacts that would take what we stole off our hands."

"But you were the boss."

"I told them I wouldn't do it unless they agreed to that. It takes brains to not get caught."

Chris was still looking confused. "Everybody thinks you're so sweet and wonderful."

Dylan bowed, but her expression was sly. "People are easy to fool. You lay your hand on your chest and tell them how gosh-darned *good* you are, and they believe it."

A story Lorilee told me after her first meeting with Dylan came to mind. "You stole money from your grandma and blamed it on Ricky."

"I didn't really *say* it was him. I let her think it *might* have been."

That brought back something else Lorilee had said. "You used Mr. Pasella's client list to find houses you could rob."

"Yup."

"But you told Ms. Pasella that Ricky and Chris asked you to show them the client files."

"I doubted she'd tell anyone and give her husband's business a black eye, but with Ricky dead, I had to protect myself."

Chris gave her a hard look. "You took my car. You drove it into that lake. You let Ricky drown."

"I didn't *let* him drown. It was an accident." For a second, she almost seemed human. "I feel really bad about it."

"How many times have you set Ricky up to take the fall if you got caught?" Birdy asked. "Did he know how little he meant to you?"

"Ricky knew the risks. He thought it was fun to get dressed in our crime scene suits and sneak around in people's houses. He was always saying we should take selfies sitting at some huge dinner table or lying on somebody's big old round bed." She raised her brows. "Being the brains and the boss, I told him that was a no-no." For a second her face softened. "We had fun on our little 'cousin excursions.' I'm going to miss that."

Birdy made a rude sound. "Like you care who gets hurt. Chris didn't do anything, and you're willing to let him take the blame for Ricky's death."

Dylan gave him a flirty glance. "What can I say? You're convenient."

"And you're rotten," Birdy shot back.

Though her anger was understandable, I wondered if Birdy realized how helpless we were. I tried to think of a different way to go. Maybe I could flatter Dylan, tell her how clever she was, and convince her we wanted to be part of her enterprise. She seemed to want people to see her as good. Maybe I could—

Dylan put an end to my vague plan. "While I'd love to stay and chat, I have to get my dad's car back home before he notices it's gone. We need to move things along."

"Should I tie them up?" Stu asked.

Dylan shook her head. "No. There can't be any evidence they were restrained."

"What do you mean?"

165

"There's going to be a suicide pact out here tonight." Dylan pointed to each of us as she explained. "Talbot here is a mess, because he knows he's going to jail. Birdy is in love with him, so she can't let him die alone." Smiling at me, she finished, "And this poor jerk lusts after Birdy, so he'll do whatever she wants."

"No one will believe I'd kill myself," I said.

"That's exactly what they'll be saying tomorrow." In a now-familiar gesture, Dylan put a hand on her chest and took on a breathless, shocked tone. "'I can't believe that weird new kid had the nerve to go through with it. It's always the quiet ones that surprise you.' You'll all be the talk of the school."

Stu seemed nervous. "You're going to kill them?" I noticed he had distanced himself from the decision.

"What else? You were supposed to scare Chris into keeping quiet, which you obviously failed to do, and he told these two about you."

"Chris didn't tell," I said. "I saw Stu threaten him, and it made me suspicious."

Dylan made a *tsk* sound. "Very sloppy, Mr. Miller. I'm not sure why I put up with you."

Stu chewed at his bottom lip. "We never killed nobody before. I mean, Ricky died, but—"

"It was an accident." Dylan's tone relieved her of all responsibility. "My ankle got twisted under the brake pedal when we hit the water. Even if I could have managed to haul him onto dry land, I'd have been seen. Screwed."

"But we don't have to *kill* them. We could—"

"What should we do, Stuart?" Dylan interrupted. "Make them pinky swear they won't tell what they know?"

"No, but—"

"You've got a record, old friend. If we're caught, I'll blame everything on you. I'll do a year in juvie and then resume my life. You'll go back to prison, and this time, it will be long-term. So you tell me, do we let them tell the cops what they know?"

Stu sighed. "How do we make it work?"

Dylan took an LED flashlight out of her jacket pocket and pointed the beam up at a loft that lined the front of the hut. "There's our scaffold. You're going to have to go somewhere and get rope."

"I've got rope in the truck, about thirty feet, I think. I use it for tying stuff down in the back." Stu seemed to have reconciled himself to the task at hand. He even sounded pleased to be able to meet Dylan's need.

"Brilliant. Climb up there and make sure there's a board strong enough to handle the weight." Dylan turned to us. "While we make the arrangements, you kids sit still and be very, very good. I've never actually fired my dad's gun before, but at this range, I probably can't miss."

Dylan shined her light for Stu as he climbed a primitive ladder at the end of the loft planking. Stepping carefully onto the platform, he examined the main cross beam. "This one's solid all the way across." When he came back down, he and Dylan stayed near the front for a few minutes, speaking in low tones. I shivered at the thought that they were deciding how to go about making our "suicides" look real.

"We need to go at them when they come back," Birdy whispered. "There's two of them and three of us."

"They have a knife and a gun," Chris objected.

"We'll do something they don't expect," I suggested. "Create confusion."

"What kind of confusion?" Birdy asked.

"I'm not sure."

Taking hold of her orange crate, Birdy scooted it back a few inches, so she sat at the very edge of the lantern's light. "When I say, 'Go!' Jesse, I want you to dive to your left. Hit the dirt and roll into the dark, so it's hard for her to get a shot at you. Chris, you do the same, only go right."

"They'll shoot us," he objected.

"They'll shoot *at* us," Birdy said. "If you keep moving, you should be okay."

"We can't outrun bullets." Chris didn't get how desperate our situation was.

"They're going to *kill* us," I told him. "Keep that in mind, and you've got nothing to lose."

I shut up then, because Dylan started back to where we sat. Behind her, the door ground on its track, and the sky outside showed as Stu left the hut. Dylan held the gun firmly in hand, but I tried to cheer myself somewhat by recalling her confession that she'd never fired one before.

Birdy had formed a plan, and while I wished I knew what it was, I trusted her. At this point, I kinda had to.

"Stu won't be long," Dylan said as if apologizing for the wait. "We'll—"

We never heard the rest, because Birdy shouted, "Go!" I dived to my left, rolling into the shadows where the lantern light didn't reach. Perhaps a half-second later, Chris did the same. Dylan made an involuntary sound of surprise and raised the gun, aiming at the spot where Chris had disappeared, and fired. Since I didn't hear Chris cry out, I hoped she'd missed.

Birdy got to her feet, but instead of diving for cover, she took a step back, planted her right leg, and sent the crate she'd been sitting on flying toward Dylan. It was an excellent example of the side kick she'd learned in soccer. Dylan ducked my way to avoid getting hit, but I was already moving forward, ready to take up the attack. Grabbing my crate, I swung it like a club, knocking Dylan to the ground. I heard the breath leave her lungs in a huff, and she lay there, trying to regain her wind. She still held onto the gun, but for the moment, she could do nothing but gasp for air.

"Go!" Birdy said. We headed for the door, which Stu had left open. Turning left, we hurtled around the corner, following our earlier path toward the back of the hut. Looking back once, I glimpsed Stu standing beside his truck, a coil of rope in hand. The overhead light reached far enough for me to see the look of confusion on his face.

Chapter Thirty-Two

Lorilee

I wandered the house like a sleepwalker, avoiding a sleeping cat here and there. Jess' text about following Birdy had made me apprehensive. He didn't own a car, and Chris didn't have his anymore. So how had they followed her? Where was this Quonset hut, and what had they found there?

Callie had gone to bed, as had the Professor. I was sure they were missing me, but— The ringtone made me jump, and when I saw *J Law* on the caller ID, my nervousness rose another notch.

"Hello, Detective."

"I got a weird call from 911 dispatch," Law said, skipping the usual pleasantries. "Where is Jesse tonight?"

When I told him, Law sighed deeply. "Why would he do something like that?"

"If a person can't prove his theory of a crime, and the police are looking in the wrong direction, he's forced to get creative."

An irritated sigh told me Law wasn't pleased with my analysis, but to his credit, he didn't argue. "I've asked the service to locate him if they can, but it isn't as easy as people think. We aren't the FBI, so our 911 doesn't automatically give a caller's location. They can usually find the cell tower that transmitted the call, but without more sophisticated equipment than we've got, we can't zero in on the phone. Hang on." A short time later he reported, "Our system shows Jess is southeast of Linville, but it's only accurate within a square mile. Can you narrow that down for us?"

"His last text said they were at an old Quonset hut. He didn't know where."

Law sighed again, deeper this time. "Okay. I'll see what I can do with that."

Going into the bedroom, I took up my tablet and turned on the light. Callie looked up, disapproving. When I didn't join her, she jumped down from the bed and stretched, extending a back leg, to show her displeasure.

"I'm worried, Cal." She didn't seem to be, but that's cats for you. As long as there's food and it isn't too cold, life is okay.

"Quonset huts in Turner County" gave me nothing. I tried "aerial photos of Turner County" and got more than I could handle. I tried "aerial photos of central western Florida" and got hundreds of pictures of the area, many showing the decimation caused by Hurricane Ian. Finally, I went back to "Quonset huts" but put neighboring counties into the search directions. On the third try, I got one. The building wasn't the focus of the photo, and the article was twenty years old, but the headline said, "Development Stalls on Plans for Former Florida Grove." It had happened fairly often in the 2000s. Buyers bought up agricultural land, intending to turn it into residential space. Then the hot property market had abruptly cooled, and many tracts were left unused. These days they were neither fish nor fowl, no longer farmland or operating orange groves, but never turned into something else.

Should I call Detective Law and tell him I'd found a possibility? Rather than delay him with conversation, I forwarded the photo to his phone with a message: *No idea if this is the place, but it's worth checking out.* Whether he could find it or not, I'd done my part.

Except it didn't feel like I had. Jess was out there, no longer communicating, possibly in danger. The only thing that kept me home was …

Nothing. I wanted to be out there, except I didn't know where "there" was.

Going back to the photo, I studied it for landmarks. Near the right border was a road, and along it was a small, wooden sign. I magnified until I could read, "Dina's Diner, 1/2 mile." Hoping that Dina was still in business, I entered the name into Google Search and got a photo of a dilapidated but still operating restaurant on Big Creek Road, which was south of Linville. In the picture, hand-lettered signs advertised boiled peanuts and key lime pie. I asked the tablet to locate the diner on a map and then zoomed in and out until I had a sense of what I was looking at. Dina's sat in the northwest section of Hardee County. To the south, the land turned to swamp. Since an orange grove wouldn't have done well in soil that moist, I concluded the Quonset hut had to sit north of the diner.

I had a road and a general location. After texting Law again to tell him what I'd discovered, I went out into the moist night air and started my car. I could have made a half-dozen mistakes in my figuring, but at least I was no longer doing nothing. I was doing my best to find Jess.

I found the road easily, and the diner sign told me I was headed in the right direction. The minute I saw the Quonset hut sitting perhaps a quarter mile down a lane on the right, I turned off my headlights. No sense announcing to whoever had come there in a black truck and a light-colored SUV that I was in the neighborhood. Driving slowly forward to minimize the noise, I stopped in the dark and regarded the scene before me.

What next?

For a moment, I doubted myself. What if the kids had come out here to attend a beer party, or whatever they call them these days, and I showed up like an overaged helicopter mom?

That thought disappeared when Stu Miller came out of the Quonset hut and headed toward a truck parked a few feet away. He seemed preoccupied, even worried. That was good, because otherwise, he might have seen my car among the orange trees. Opening the passenger side door of his truck, he rummaged behind the seat for something.

What should I do? Getting out of my car was a bad idea, since I wasn't exactly fleet of foot. Still, I had a sense of dread, a feeling that the kids needed me to do something. I sent a text to Law. *I'm here. It's the right place.*

Stu found what he was looking for, but as he closed the truck door, Chris shot out the open doorway of the building. A second later Jess and Birdy followed, holding hands and staggering a little in their need for speed. When a loud noise disturbed the quiet of the night, I realized that someone was shooting at them.

The kids disappeared along the side of the hut. In the doorway, a young woman appeared, holding a pistol. I squinted, unwilling to believe my eyes. Dylan? With a gun?

Stu hurried over and said something that caused her to nod. She handed him the gun, and he started around the building after the kids.

I needed to do something. Now.

Chapter Thirty-Three

Jess

We ran, stumbled, and crawled through the trees and undergrowth beside the old building. At one point, Birdy jerked to a stop, groaned softly, and let go of my hand. It felt like I'd been abandoned, but after a second, I understood. It was hard enough navigating the overgrown terrain quietly and in the dark without trying to hold on to each other. I went on, using both hands to push tree branches out of my way. Crouching low, we kept going … to where? We didn't know what lay ahead. We only knew that behind us was trouble. Dylan, Stu, or both were sure to come after us. They had weapons; we didn't. They probably knew the terrain; we didn't. They were playing for high stakes. With what we knew, they couldn't afford to let us go.

A huge crash sounded at the front of the building, followed by a scream, a moan, and a lot of rattling that made no sense at the time. I almost ran into Birdy, who had stopped short and turned toward the sound. The side of her forehead looked dark, but it might have been a shadow.

"What was that?" Chris whispered from somewhere up ahead.

"Shh!"

A second later, Stu's voice sounded behind us. "Dylan? What happened?"

He got no answer.

Birdy whispered, her lips at my ear, "I'll distract Stu. You and Chris take him down."

"You can't—"

"Do it!"

I was beginning to realize that Birdy could be a little bossy.

A second later, she spoke in a completely different voice, high and trembling. "Guys, where are you?"

We didn't answer, but Stu's voice came closer, and he said, "Hey, little lady. Did your friends run off and leave you?"

"I think so." Birdy sounded tearful. "Look, I won't tell anybody what happened here tonight, okay? I just want to—"

"Don't worry, little girl. Everything's going to be okay."

Stu didn't sound the least bit sincere, but the conversation helped me home in on his position. Quietly, very quietly, I circled back the way I'd come. Birdy helped by stepping away each time Stu got close to her. She appeared to be crying, and she kept saying things like, "I don't trust you," and "I'm scared." He focused on convincing her he wouldn't hurt her, probably assuming that once he had Birdy, he could force Chris and me to come back.

Finally I saw Stu silhouetted against the metal side of the Quonset hut. I went on through the trees until I was directly behind him. Thoughts went through my head like little arrows, piercing the bubble of confidence I tried to create. He might shoot Birdy. He might move at just the moment I made my attack. He might hear me behind him, turn, and shoot me.

I told myself I had to be fearless, like Bruiser, who never let anything as wispy as "might" or "maybe" stop him. Taking a big breath, I launched myself forward like a missile, aiming high to knock Stu off balance. When I connected, he staggered forward but didn't go down right away. Then his foot caught on something, a root or a rock, and we both hit the dirt. Stu swore as he lost hold of his flashlight, which skittered into the foliage, spun halfway around, and stopped. Somehow, he managed to hold onto the gun. Seeing that, I grabbed his arm and tried to pin it down. Stu twisted under me, trying desperately to flip our positions. Since he had fifty pounds on me and I knew exactly zero wrestling moves, it was only a matter of time until he succeeded.

Then someone landed on both of us. I'd started to push myself up to my knees, but I went down again, dealing Stu a blow that made him grunt and swear even worse than before.

"You good?" Chris said in my ear.

"Yeah," I managed. Stu started struggling again, so I punched him below the ribcage with my free hand, hitting as hard as I could from my awkward position. He groaned and went slack, but I doubted he was finished. Where was the gun? Though I couldn't see it, I kept pressure on the arm with my left hand and pushed his head down with my right, hoping he couldn't fire at us with his arm and his face pushed into the ground.

"Pin his legs down," I told Chris, and he did, securing Stu's bottom half with his weight. Realizing he couldn't dislodge two people, Stu sort of deflated and stopped struggling. That was good, because I needed a minute. As I caught my breath, Stu's flashlight levitated from its spot and turned toward us, lighting the scene. Stu lay on his belly. I sprawled across his shoulders sideways, and Chris sat on his feet. Birdy stood over us all, holding the gun she'd apparently ripped from Stu's hand during our impromptu wrestling match.

"Stay here," she ordered, handing Chris the light. "I'm going to see what that noise was out front."

Both of us said, "No," but Birdy was already gone.

"What should we do?" I asked.

Chris made an irritated huff. "We get this guy taken care of and hope your girlfriend knows what she's doing,"

Chapter Thirty-Four

Lorilee

When Jesse, Chris, and Birdy disappeared into the trees, I hesitated, trying to decide what to do. Should I roll down the window and inform Stu Miller that the police were on their way? Should I pretend to be an irritated landowner and order them off the property?

Neither seemed likely to work. Stu had a gun, and he'd gone after the kids. The only way to stop him was to create a distraction that demanded his attention.

Without giving myself time to think, I rammed my car into gear, turned on the headlights, and floored the gas pedal. Dylan, who still stood at the front of the Quonset hut, looked up in terror as I approached. Though I had no intention of running her down, she dived out of the way.

When my car hit the hut, many things happened all at once. The wooden end wall gave and splintered. The metal cover vibrated. The whole structure shook. My engine died. The air bags deployed, giving me the sensation that I'd been kicked by a strong but very fluffy bunny. When the noises and the unfamiliar sensations stopped, I needed a few seconds to recall where I was and what I'd done. I climbed out of the car, shaken but not seriously hurt.

Dylan lay on the ground to my left. Diving to escape what she'd seen as my attack, she'd landed in a pile of ancient orange crates. They'd cracked and shifted under her weight, until she was almost hidden from sight. She squealed and batted at them as the splintery edges poked and scraped her.

Leaning over her, I asked, "Are you hurt?"

"You broke my arm!" she howled. I might have felt sorry for her ... until the cursing started.

At that moment Birdy appeared, panting with effort and holding the gun with both hands, as if it might try to jump out of her grip. "Now honestly, Dylan," she said as she raised it, "I've actually never fired a gun before, but don't even think about trying anything. At this range, I probably can't miss."

"Jess? Chris?" I asked.

"Back there. They got Stu, and I got his gun."

"The police are on their way." Birdy nodded but remained intent on keeping Dylan where she was. Hoping she was right about the boys being okay, I went along the side of the building. A flashlight glowed up ahead, and I said, "Jess, are you back there?"

"I'm here, Lorilee. Chris too. We're okay. Are things good out front?"

"Birdy has the situation in hand," I said as the wail of sirens rose in the distance. "But I'm afraid my car will never be the same."

Chapter Thirty-Five

Lorilee

I suggested Jess take some time off from school, saying I'd excuse him for the rest of the week. He wasn't the type who liked attention, so the hoopla sure to result when the news came out about Dylan and her gang would embarrass and distress him. He replied that he didn't want to miss his group project presentation in science on Friday, since they'd put so much work into it. "We learned," he told me, "that the more the manufacturer hypes a drink, the worse it's likely to be for you."

I snickered. "Why do you think we see so many ads for beer and soda pop? Same principle."

He did take one day off, which I thought was good. Anyone who's been through a frightening experience knows it takes time to process it. That afternoon, I saw Jess sitting on a post at the turnaround, talking to Chris. I figured they were working through their trauma together.

Birdy and Dylan both spent the night in the hospital, Dylan with a broken ulna and under arrest, and Birdy with a possible concussion from whacking her head on a tree branch in the dark. In all the excitement, she'd ignored the blood running down the side of her face. The doctor said keeping her overnight was mostly a precaution, and she would likely be released in the morning.

We'd all been checked out by paramedics. Three of us, Jess, Chris, and I, were deemed fit, so we were questioned by Detective Law and then allowed to follow Birdy to the hospital. Surprisingly, my car, though mangled in front, was operational. Law had a deputy follow us into town to make sure we made it.

As we waited outside the emergency room, Birdy's stepfather came in, his face pinched with concern. I explained the situation as best I could, weaving together what the boys had told me.

"She was trying to keep Rooster out of trouble." Mr. Kalamaris shook his head. "My boy don't make good decisions a lot of the time, but Birdy does her best to keep him honest." With a grim smile he added, "I think maybe she doesn't want me to have to deal with his foolishness. Birdy's a good girl, and he don't deserve a sister like her."

"I don't think your son did anything wrong," I said. "It must have been a big temptation though, money and adventure all rolled in together."

"I'll give him adventure," Kalamaris muttered darkly. "He can go to work for my brother at the car wash and *earn* his spending money."

I had a visit from Detective Law the day after the adventure. When I saw his car pull in, I feared Jess or I or both of us was in for another "stay out of police business" talk. Instead, Law was in the mood to tell me what he guessed I was dying to know. "I can't say much, and I hope you don't pass this on," he said after I'd provided sugar cookies and unsweet iced tea. "Our psychologist says that girl Dylan is a bona fide criminal sociopath. Not all sociopaths break the law, but her kind will do anything to get what they want. She's honestly surprised that we don't understand."

I shivered. "She would have murdered three of her schoolmates."

Law smiled grimly. "That didn't bother her, but it bothered old Stu. He's willing to tell us anything we want to know to keep us from lumping him in with her."

"Would he have gone through with killing them, do you think?"

"I don't know. He claims he was trying to figure out a way to let them escape, but the girl was right. Now that he's caught, he'll go to prison for a long time. It's hard to say what he'd have done if they hadn't taken off."

I shook my head. "I can't get over Dylan as a murderer. She's still a child."

"A really nasty one, you ask me."

"I spoke with her great-grandmother once. She thought she was wonderful."

"That's the sociopath thing, I guess. They schmooze their way through, and people think they're all sweetness and light."

"Didn't anyone notice that she wasn't?"

"A couple of her teachers saw glimmers of evil behind that smile of hers, but aside from noting it in her file—one teacher called her "duplicitous"—nothing ever came of it. I think Dylan was able to hide behind her cousin Ricky's more overt misbehavior. He probably took the blame for a lot of things she did, or maybe thought up."

"What will happen to her?"

He looked disgusted. "My guess? She'll lower her head and shed a tear and promise to do better, and some judge will give her community service. Stu will take most of the blame, even though he was basically her flunky."

"Well, you did your part. You caught them."

"With your help." He took a long sip of tea. "I'm sorry I was slow to believe you about young Talbot. I should have—" His face broke into a sheepish grin. "Honestly, that pushy mother of his made me kind of bull-headed about it. She said I was wrong, so I wanted her to be." His expression turned rueful. "My wife used to say I could be that way with irritating people."

I hoped I wasn't one of those in the detective's mind. "You were there when we needed you," I told him. "That's all we can ask."

That afternoon, when Mitzi returned from picking Greg up from school, she didn't turn in at her drive but stopped outside mine. Hearing the horn beep, I went outside. When Mitzi gestured for me to come out to the road I did, but with some trepidation.

The passenger side window was rolled down, and an angry-looking Greg sat facing the windshield, his chin and lower lip jutted.

"Lorilee, Greggy has something to say to you." I waited, but he didn't move. "Greggy, I know you've been spying on Ms. Riley. That is not nice."

Not nice? She'd done it for months before Art Fusilli ordered her to stop.

"Lorilee, Chris is very grateful for all you and Jesse did to help him prove his innocence. He tells me that Greg has been harassing you, and he wants it to stop."

"She's got a bunch of cats in there," Greg said between clenched teeth. "At least twelve. Maybe more."

"Greg, I won't tolerate you lying about Ms. Riley. She wrecked her beautiful car to save your brother, and Chris says he knows for a fact she hasn't got a single extra cat. Now say you're sorry."

We both waited. It was a long wait, but finally the kid opened his lips enough to say, "Sorry."

"Now that wasn't so hard, was it?" She patted her son's shoulder, which might have been made of stone for all the response she got. "We should always tell the truth, because it makes everything better. Momma has the respect of the police, because they realize now that I told them the truth about Chris the whole time. Am I right, Lorilee?"

If I wanted to kill myself, Mitzi, I'd climb up your ego and jump to your IQ.

"Absolutely." Bending close to Greg's face, I said, "You have a nice day now, *Greggy.*"

Back inside, I saw that I had a text from Dr. Ahuja. He'd found out that Poor Kitty's owner died when the hurricane flattened her house. Relatives had notified the shelter that none of them wanted the old woman's cat.

"This one's ours now," I told Jess when he came into the house. "You haven't had the chance to officially name a pet so far, so I'll leave it up to you."

"Easy," he replied. "Birdy's reading *The Hunchback of Notre Dame*, and she mentioned a name I liked. Esmeralda."

"Like an emerald. With eyes like hers, that's perfect," I said.

It's a little long, I thought, *but we can shorten it to Esmé.*

ABOUT THE AUTHOR

Maggie Pill is also Peg Herring, but Maggie's much younger and cooler.

Visit http://maggiepill.maggiepillmysteries.com.

or https://www.pegherring.com/for more great mysteries.

Books available in print, e-book, & (usually) audio from major booksellers. Or ask for it at your local library.

The Sleuth Sisters Series—follow sisters Barb, Faye, and Retta as they start a detective agency, hoping to overcome middle-aged stagnation. Each sister has talents and...eccentricities: Barb sneaks out at night and corrects mistakes on local signs; Faye would try to pet a wolverine (if Michigan had any); and Retta is used to getting her own way because she's just so cute.

Book #1- *The Sleuth Sisters*

Book #2- *3 Sleuths, 2 Dogs, 1 Murder*

Book #3- *Murder in the Boonies*

Book #4- *Sleuthing at Sweet Springs*

Book #5- *Eat, Drink, and Be Wary*

Book #6- *Peril, Plots, and Puppies*

Book #7- *Captured, Escape, Repeat*

Trailer Park Tales – Couples at the Beautiful Bird RV Park enjoy Florida's warmth all winter long, but they can't stop investigating crimes that disturb the peace of the park.

Book #1- *Once Upon a Trailer Park*

Book #2- *Twice the Crime This Time*

Book #3-*Third Crime's the Charm*

Cats & Crimes-Lorilee Riley might not be young and agile anymore, but she knows a lot about cats and a little about people, which is helpful when solving crimes.

Book #1 *Cats and Crimes*

BOOKS BY PEG HERRING

The Simon & Elizabeth Mysteries *(Tudor Era Historical)*
Book #1- *Her Highness' First Murder*
Book #2- *Poison, Your Grace*
Book #3- *The Lady Flirts with Death*
Book #4- *Her Majesty's Mischief*
***

The Loser Mysteries *(Contemporary Mystery/Suspense)*
Book #1- *Killing Silence*
Book #2 -*Killing Memories*
Book #3- *Killing Despair*
***

Clan Macbeth Historical Romance (*medieval Scotland*)
Book #1-*Macbeth's Niece*
Book #2- *Double Toil & Trouble*
***

Mercedes Mysteries *(Modern Suspense with Historical Elements)*
Book #1- *Shakespeare's Blood*
Book #2- *Charlie Dickens' Documents*
***

Kidnap Capers (*Thrillers with Cozy Tendencies*)
Book #1- *KIDNAP.org*
Book #2- *Pharma Con*
Book #3- *The Trouble with Dad*
***

Standalone Mysteries
Somebody Doesn't Like Sarah Leigh (Contemporary Cozy Mystery)
Her Ex-GI P.I. ('60s-era mystery)
Not Dead Yet... ('60s-era paranormal mystery)
***

Women's Fiction
Deceiving Elvera-Two women meet on Michigan's Mackinac Island. They begin a lifelong friendship, but it ends when they face danger and betrayal on Thailand's eastern border.

Sister Saint, Sister Sinner-Ruth has hopes of being First Lady of the United States. Her sister Kim is coping with divorce and senses she's floating listlessly through life. Third sister Nettie has committed a murder she will neither excuse nor explain.

CPSIA information can be obtained
at www.ICGtesting.com
Printed in the USA
BVHW031722140623
665957BV00001B/18